When not teaching or writing, **Anne Oliver** loves nothing more than escaping into a book. She keeps a box of tissues handy—her favourite stories are intense, passionate, against-all-odds romances. Eight years ago she began creating her own characters in paranormal and time travel adventures, before turning to contemporary romance. Other interests include quilting, astronomy, all things Scottish, and eating anything she doesn't have to cook. Sharing her characters' journeys with readers all over the world is a privilege…and a dream come true. The winner of Australia's Romantic Book of the Year Award for short category in both 2007 and 2008, Anne lives in Adelaide, South Australia, and has two adult children.

Visit her website at www.anne-oliver.com. She loves to hear from readers. Email her at anne@anne-oliver.com

With thanks to my editor, Meg Lewis.

For my colleagues and friends who supported me through tough times during the writing of this book, especially Gay—thanks for the roses!

The ultimate kings of seduction!

THE PLAYBOYS
AND HEROES
COLLECTION

The Playboys and Heroes large print collection
gives you lavish stories of luxury
from your favourite top authors
in easier-to-read print.

AT HIS SERVICE: MEMOIRS OF A MILLIONAIRE'S MISTRESS

Anne Oliver

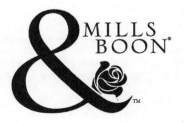

First published in Great Britain 2009
by Mills & Boon, an imprint of Harlequin (UK) Limited,
Large Print edition 2013
Harlequin (UK) Limited,
Eton House, 18-24 Paradise Road, Richmond, Surrey TW9 1SR

© Anne Oliver 2009

ISBN: 978 0 263 23631 6

Harlequin (UK) policy is to use papers that are natural, renewable and recyclable products and made from wood grown in sustainable forests. The logging and manufacturing process conform to the legal environmental regulations of the country of origin.

Printed and bound in Great Britain
by CPI Antony Rowe, Chippenham, Wiltshire

CHAPTER ONE

'DON'T date this man.'

Didi O'Flanagan paid scant attention to her workmate's warning, barely glancing up as she scoured her bag for lip gloss. 'Whatever he did, Roz, he probably doesn't deserve to have his photo plastered to the mirror in a public restroom...' Her words segued to a hum of approval, lip gloss momentarily forgotten.

Maybe he did deserve it. His eyes—deep dark blue—were the kind of eyes that could persuade you to do things you'd never do in your right mind...

'Only the woman who put it here knows that.' Roz leaned in for a closer look. 'You must've really ticked her off, Cameron Black. Still, you are a bit of a hunk.'

'Yeah...' Didi had to agree. Dark hair, squared jaw. Perfect kissing lips. What did the rest of him look like? she wondered. She imagined a man with looks like that would keep his body toned to match. In fact she could imagine quite a lot about that body. 'We could try Googling those "don't date him" websites...'

'Hmm, revenge. Undoubtedly a dish best served online...' Roz agreed. 'But right now, if we want to keep our jobs, we'd better get out there and start serving those impatient big-shots,' Roz reminded her, heading for the door.

Didi blinked, feeling as if she'd somehow stepped out of a time warp. 'Right behind you.'

Cameron Black. Why did that name sound familiar? Didi wondered. Shaking the thought away for now, she unscrewed her tube of colour, slicked coral gloss over her lips.

She twitched at a few blonde spikes, straightened her uniform's little bow tie and fiddled with her name-tag, which always seemed to tilt at an angle no matter how many times she adjusted it.

She couldn't resist; her gaze slid back to the printout on the mirror. Below the picture were the words, 'He's not the man you think he is.' On impulse, she reached out. She didn't care what he'd done, it wasn't right. That was what she told herself as she peeled it off. There were two sides to every story. Not that she knew much about relationships. In her twenty-three years there'd been only one serious relationship, and that mistake had coloured her perception in a very *un*colourful way.

But she couldn't bring herself to crumple the paper and toss it in the waste basket on her way out as she'd intended. It seemed a sacrilege to spoil that perfect face. She folded it into quarters, then again, carefully creasing the lines before sliding it into the pocket of her black trousers.

A few moments later Didi circulated the crowded room with her tray of finger food. Predominantly male executives in business attire made for a sea of sombre suits interspersed with splashes of colour and the occasional whiff of feminine perfume.

Didi aimed a winning smile at the group of men she'd targeted as being the head honchos. 'Would you like to try a crab cake with lemongrass sauce? Or perhaps one of these baked cheese olive balls?'

As expected, her smile was ignored as they continued their discussion around the model of a proposed development for one of Melbourne's inner city precincts on a table in front of them, but a few greedy fingers plucked her dainty morsels off the tray.

Rude, rude, rude. Her smile remained, but in-

side she gritted her teeth as she skirted the group
to reappear around the other side. She hated this
subservient, thankless job. But right now she had
no alternative if she didn't want to slink home to
Sydney and admit she'd made a mistake—

'Thank you, Didi.'

The unexpected rich baritone voice had her
looking up—way up—at the man who'd taken
the last crab cake *and* had the courtesy to use her
name. 'You're welcome. I hope you enjoy…it…'
Her voice faded away as her gaze met a pair of
twinkling blue eyes…

This couldn't be the man whose photo was
warming her right hip even as he smiled. Could it?

Yes. It could—and it most definitely was. So
the woman who'd left the picture in the Ladies
had known he'd be here—maybe she still was,
and wanted to witness his humiliation.

The cheap printout didn't do him justice—he
was *gorgeous.* His eyes were navy, almost black.
And focused wholly on her. He'd shaved tonight;
no sign of that stubble. Just smooth tanned skin…
Her palms itched to find out just how smooth.
The maroon and black tie's sheen accentuated
his snowy white shirt, drawing her attention to
a prominent Adam's apple and solid neck. His

hair was shorter than it was in the picture and the room's light caught threads of auburn amongst the brown.

He wore a pinstriped charcoal suit and she knew from her experience with fabrics that it was Italian and expensive. Touchable. Warm from his body heat. Her insides did a slow roll and her fingers tightened on the tray.

As she watched he lifted the crab cake to his lips before popping it into his mouth, still smiling at her, and for an instant she bathed in the warmth before he turned away.

No. She wanted to bask in that heat a moment longer. 'You forgot to dip,' she found herself saying. Loudly. Too loudly. His gaze swung back. 'And that was the last one...' She trailed off, lost for a moment in his eyes.

His lips stretched into a smile as he continued chewing. She had a completely inappropriate image of dipping her fingers in the sauce then sliding them between his lips, and her pulse quickened.

'That's too bad,' he said, his voice a tone or two lower, his eyes a tad darker. As if he was sharing the same fantasy. 'It was delicious nevertheless.'

'Try a cheese and olive ball.' She offered her

tray up like some kind of entreaty. 'It's a different texture but if you like olives—' Cheeks heating, she caught her runaway tongue between her lips to stem the verbal tide. *What the heck was she doing?*

'I love olives.' He selected one, his gaze once again focused on her, warming her from the inside out.

'When you've quite finished.' A man with thick white hair aimed his glare at her over the rim of a pair of butt-ugly spectacles. 'As I was saying, Cam...'

Cam held Didi's eyes for a second longer, then gave a conspiratorial wink before getting back to business.

Cam... *Cameron Black.* Didi mentally repeated his name as she watched one long tapered finger touch the model of his proposed development as he spoke. What would it feel like to have that finger touch her? Anywhere. For any reason...

Get real, she admonished herself. *Step away before you make a complete and utter fool of yourself.*

This man was into property deals and big-business networking. He didn't have time for the simpler things like social conversation. No doubt he spent his entire life dealing with men like Mr White Hair. He was one of those men for whom making money was more important than relationships—hence the poster, no doubt.

As she stepped back she couldn't help noticing the arched façade of the model he was touching. She frowned, squinting without her glasses. It looked like her apartment building.

It *was* her apartment building. They'd been served with eviction notices months ago, but Didi hadn't got around to finding herself a new place yet. At least not one she could afford.

Resentment simmered beneath her carefully cultivated waitress persona. *That* was where she'd seen his name. Cameron Black Property Developers were kicking her out along with several other families in three weeks; she'd seen the signage on the vacant lot next door where a pawn shop and a sleazy tattoo parlour had recently been demolished. All destined to be part of a new complex that would take months to complete.

A different kind of heat fired through her veins. The burn of disappointment, anger. Outrage. Greed was Cameron's motivation. Certainly not concern for the residents who couldn't afford to move to the more upmarket parts of town.

She should bite her tongue, turn around and head to the kitchen to refill her depleted tray. But she'd never been one who could keep her mouth shut. 'Excuse me.'

Six heads turned, six pairs of eyes drilled into hers, but it was Cameron Black she focused on. 'Have you given any thought to the tenants you're turfing out at number two hundred and three?'

His jaw firmed, the warmth in his eyes vanished. 'I beg your pardon?'

She waved a hand over the model. 'I don't know how people like you sleep at night.' She scoffed out a humourless laugh. 'Mrs Jacobs has been there for fifteen years—she's had to go to Geelong to live with her daughter's family. And Clem Mason's—'

'Watch yourself, girlie,' Mr White Hair warned.

Fired up now, Didi didn't spare him a glance. 'Do you know how hard it is to find suitable accommodation at affordable rates, Mr Black? Do you care at all about the ordinary people trying to get by on the basics who live—make that *lived*—in that building?'

'I'm not aware of any problems.' His voice was cool professionalism.

'Of course you're not.' And he'd probably trotted

out that same line to the pinner-upper of the photo in her pocket. She could only shake her head on behalf of women everywhere. 'Maybe that's why you're the current Pin-Up Boy in the ladies' loo.' Her voice carried way further than she'd meant it to and a hush descended around them like a suffocating shroud.

Twin spots of colour slashed Cameron Black's cheeks and his mouth opened as if to speak, but she turned away, her runaway tongue cleaving to the roof of her mouth. Before she made matters worse, she set her tray on a nearby table and quickly made her way towards the restroom.

She pushed through the door, found it empty and leaned back against its solid barrier with a heartfelt sigh. Tonight her mouth might just have cost her this job.

She stepped to the vanity counter and turned on the tap, dabbing her neck with cold water. Thankless or not, she needed this work. Why couldn't she control her tongue? And why did the man-to-die-for have to be her evil landlord?

The door swung open with a whoosh, pushed wide by a very tanned, very firm, very *masculine* hand. Didi's breath snagged in her chest. Then she steeled herself to meet Cameron Black's grim reflection in the mirror.

Instead of feeling threatened, she felt...anticipation. It buzzed through her body, turning her legs to liquid and drawing her nipples into tight points of sensation. *Damn him,* she didn't want to feel as if she were poised and breathless on the edge of a lava pit. She wanted to get herself together, and how could she do that when he'd invaded the only place she'd thought safe?

She turned so that she could meet him face to face on equal terms, gripping her fingers on the counter top at her sides for support. Except he had a good fourteen inches on her. Struggling to keep the nerves from her voice, she lifted her chin and met his gaze. 'I think you made a wrong turn somewhere.'

'Not me. You.' His gaze darkened, indigo satin over hot coals, and his voice was silky smooth when he advised, 'You really shouldn't bad-mouth the people who help contribute to your pay at the end of the evening.'

How was it that even though his eyes remained fused with hers he managed to conjure a shimmer of heat up the entire length of her body as if he'd swept a hand from ankle to clavicle and every place in between?

She shook her head. 'I tell the truth, Mr Black. Unfortunately the truth often gets me in trouble...'

When his gaze finally released her he scanned the room. 'And how do you know my name?'

She arched a brow. 'I'd suggest most of the women at this function know your name by now.'

His eyes narrowed. The door swung closed behind him, swirling the air and leaving the two of them alone. The scent of his cologne reached her nostrils in the draught he'd created. Without thought she breathed deep, inhaling its fragrance: snowflakes on cedar-wood. As if by some force she didn't know she had, it seemed to draw him closer. It seemed to draw the walls in, suck the air away, until he was standing so close she could feel his body heat through the fine-textured weave of his shirt.

He placed his hands firmly on the counter top, a fingerprint away from hers, boxing her in. 'What game are you playing at—' and even though she was certain he remembered her name, his gaze slid over the swell of her left breast where her name-tag hung at its permanent forty-five-degree angle '—Didi?'

She slid an unsteady hand into her trouser pocket, the backs of her fingers bumping against his and sending fireworks shooting up her arm in the process, and pulled out the folded sheet of paper, thrust it at his chest. 'It's not my game.'

Straightening, he unfolded it and scanned the contents. She watched his jaw bunch, his knuckles whiten on the paper. In the silence that followed she could hear the quickened rasp of his breathing, could almost feel his anger as a third entity in the room with them.

'I found it on the mirror.'

She flinched again when he closed a substantial fist around it, crumpled it beyond redemption with an impatient crackle, then shoved it in his pocket. She had to bite her lip to stop herself from asking for it back. Of course she wanted it back...so she could grind her heel into his face when she left her flat in three weeks' time with nowhere to live.

'Thank you,' he said quietly. 'I've been having some trouble with an ex girlfriend.'

'No kidding. Did you kick her out too?'

'As a matter of fact it was she who did the kicking.'

She was tempted to dole out more sarcasm but

the complete lack of emotion in his expression stopped her—too complete. Too controlled. He'd blocked the pain, she thought, and stuffed her hands into her trouser pockets to curb her natural instinct to reach out to him. He was hurting, and she understood too well how it felt to be tossed aside. 'Yeah, well, you're better off without someone like that.'

And I'm better off not knowing. She needed to remember who he was: *Evil Landlord.* He might be hot sex in a pinstripe suit but his motive in life was greed. Keeping her backside against the counter top, she sidled closer to the door—she had to get out before she changed her mind and offered something stupid, like sympathy. Or sex on the vanity unit.

Cam sensed her imminent departure but he wasn't done with her. He slammed his hands back on the tiles on either side of hers. Wide and wary silver eyes snapped to his. She was petite. Dainty. But he knew the aura of fragility was purely that—an aura. He liked that about her—a woman with guts in a compact little package.

She'd furrowed hands through her gelled hair and it stood up now in spiky disarray. With her name-tag askew and resting on one small pert breast, she reminded him of a rather untidy pixie. The jolt of attraction was swift and unexpected. And hot.

He gritted his teeth and forced himself to focus. 'Do you want to come with me now and voice your concerns about the new development to the rest of the investors?'

'With that irritable and arrogant old man? No point. More important, I've still got half an hour of paid employment to go and, unlike *some,* I need the money.' She made a noise of disgust and her breasts rose as she drew in a short sharp breath. 'It's people like you who barge in and buy up big, ripping up homes and businesses and lives and call it "development" when in reality it's just a money-grabbing venture.'

'It's not—'

'People like *you,*' she interrupted, 'wouldn't understand the first thing about people from the other side of the tracks.'

He had a fleeting but graphic image of a past he'd spent half his life trying to forget and his gut clenched. He pushed back from the counter, his fingers tightening into fists at his sides as he remembered how long and hard he'd fought to earn the wealth and respect he now enjoyed. 'You know nothing about me.'

She waved an accusatory hand at the peach-coloured sofa. 'You followed me in *here,* didn't you? That tells me something, and, let me tell *you,* it's not flattering.'

Her eyes flashed at him, a silver blowtorch, all heat and sparks and energy, setting spot fires snapping to life through his veins. In his thirty-two years no woman had ever ignited such a reaction in him.

If he could direct that passion elsewhere... His groin tightened at the thought of where he could direct that delicate-looking hand with its clear varnished nails... 'Tell me something else, Didi. Why did you fold my picture with such obvious care and put it in your pocket? Why not throw it in the waste bin?'

Her cheeks turned a delicious shade of pink and her gaze dropped to her shoes. 'I...wasn't thinking.' Then she pushed, her palm hitting him firmly mid-chest. 'Now move.'

Her touch was like a brand, searing his flesh. Heat radiated throughout his body and his first instinct was to cover that small hand with his and keep her there just a few more seconds and argue that she *was,* in fact, thinking. About him.

But he stepped aside, the imprint of her hand still burning, and watched her march the two steps to the door, yank it open. If he wasn't wrong, those rosy cheeks gave her away. *Attraction.* And right now she was about to walk. He should be relieved—he didn't need the distraction; he certainly didn't intend dating her. So why he found himself asking for her phone number was beyond his comprehension.

She paused mid-stride, her fingers curved around the door frame, her eyes barely meeting his. 'Why?'

'I may decide to press charges against my ex.'

She scoffed and resumed walking. 'You can do that without my help.'

He stood a moment, breathing in the sweet nutty fragrance she'd left behind, feeling oddly put out. 'Damn right, Didi. I don't need your help.' *I certainly don't need you.*

He'd barely moved when her elfin face reappeared around the door. 'What makes you think I'd want to help you?' she continued as if she'd never left. 'Maybe she did us girls a favour. Apparently you're not the man she thought you were.'

She looked him up and down thoroughly from his now sweat-damp brow to his black Italian leather shoes and he had the disturbing sensation she wasn't looking at his clothes. 'Makes one wonder what she meant considering you're on the wrong side of the door here. Perhaps she knows something the rest of us girls don't.'

He didn't bother with a reply. *Didi* whoever-she-was could imply whatever the hell she liked; Cam knew exactly what Katrina had meant.

When Didi arrived home she knew she'd made the right choice in not giving Cameron Black her phone number. He was the single most dangerous man she'd ever met. He owned her apartment. He was going to tear it down.

And she had the worst case of lust for him that she'd ever experienced. How dumb was that?

Still in her coat, she was stepping out of her shoes when her mobile rang. She froze momentarily, then coughed out a laugh. Of course it couldn't be him... Pulling her phone out of her bag, she checked caller ID, breathed a sigh of relief, but only for an instant because her friend Donna was on her own with a toddler and it was well past midnight.

'Donna, what's up?'

'I've broken my leg...' Distress tightened her voice. 'Trent's not home for another two weeks and I've got no one to help look after Fraser. Can you come?'

Didi rubbed her tired eyes. Donna lived in the Yarra Valley, a couple of hours' drive from Melbourne—too far for Didi to commute on a daily basis with her unreliable car.

They'd met as volunteers at a kids' breakfast club in Sydney, then Donna had married and moved to Victoria with her husband, but he worked on an offshore oil rig half the time. Didi would have to stay with her, which meant she'd be unavailable for work—if she still had a job, that was.

She glanced at her chaotic apartment and empty cartons. If you couldn't help a friend in need... 'I'll be there as soon as I can.'

Didi threw a handful of clothes and essentials into a couple of canvas supermarket bags. At least she'd managed to pack away her precious art supplies. She still had three weeks before she had to vacate—cutting it fine, but it couldn't be helped. She wasn't about to let Donna down—Cameron Black and his big bad bulldozer would just have to wait.

* * *

Cameron wasn't sure which got to him more. The fact that Katrina had stalked him to a business function and left her poison, or that someone— a very appealing someone called Didi—had announced the fact to him at a crucial moment in negotiations.

Negotiating with Bill Smith needed subtlety and diplomacy. And as much as the man pained him, Cam needed Bill's support to help smooth things over with the council. He might have had that support sooner if Didi O'Flanagan hadn't announced Cam's poster-boy status along with her condemnation of Cameron Black Property Developers. He'd had to schedule another meeting he didn't have time for, but he'd won the older man over at least.

He stared out of his office window with its view of Telstra Stadium and the Yarra River. Didi O'Flanagan. It had been a simple matter to access her phone number through the rental agency that serviced the building and cross-reference it with the catering firm he always used. Apparently it hadn't taken Bill long either because when he'd rung they assured Cam she was no longer working with their company and did Cam wish to file a complaint as well?

Of course the name rang a bell—she lived in the building she'd been fighting for. It was due for major renovation in two weeks. They'd been served eviction notices as soon as the project had been finalised months ago. And they'd all vacated the premises except for Miss O'Flanagan in apartment six.

He expelled a long breath. She didn't deserve to lose her job for having the guts to stand up for her beliefs, however misguided they were in this particular circumstance. And she'd done him a favour by removing his photo. She obviously cared about others and respected their rights—even his, he thought, with a wry twist of his lips.

He wanted a chance to explain his vision for the development and the reasons behind it. If she'd stop for one second and listen, that was. As for living arrangements…maybe he could speed things up if she was having trouble finding a place. Find her an apartment in one of his complexes somewhere.

On the other side of the city.

The warning rang in his head. Yeah. The further away, the better.

Because he had a feeling this little pixie could

run amok over his well-ordered life—the life he'd built from scratch—with just one look from her silver eyes or one word from that tempt-me mouth.

CHAPTER TWO

Two weeks later

IT WAS a night for disasters.

Rain pelted the pavement, but that was Melbourne.

Didi's apartment building was all locked up—*one week early*—and that was entirely Cameron Black's work and the reason she now huddled on the front steps thinking of ways she might enjoy killing him. Slowly. *After* she got her stuff out.

She'd had to abandon her excuse for a car on the other side of the city with some sort of mechanical failure that no one was willing to look at until tomorrow. Not that she had any hope of paying for repairs since she'd learned she was now unemployed when she'd rung to explain why she wouldn't be able to work for the next couple of weeks.

So she considered the fact that she'd managed the rest of the way by public transport with a bag of clothing and a box of abandoned and distressed young cat she'd found beside a public toilet block a minor miracle.

Only to find herself locked out of her own apartment.

And she couldn't ring anyone from here because in her rush to help Donna she'd left her mobile behind in her apartment somewhere. She'd had to make do with Donna's landline for the past two weeks.

The busy inner suburban street was awash with wet colour, the untidy web of overhead cables dripped moisture. Trams jostled amongst the steady stream of vehicles on their way home, pedestrians huddled under umbrellas, and the aroma of Asian takeaway steamed the air. She'd kill for a fried rice about now.

At least it was relatively dry here on the top step—an awning shielded her from the worst of the weather. She pulled out the tuna sandwiches she'd bought earlier, feeding the cat tiny portions through a peephole she'd created in the side of the box. Sometime soon she was going to have to find somewhere for the little guy to pee.

'It'll be okay, Charlie,' she said, popping a bite into her own mouth, feeling more and more incensed with every passing minute. 'It's just you and me against the world and we're not going down without a fight.'

Finally. Cam came to an abrupt stop on the pavement and watched Didi from beneath his large black umbrella. She gazed up at the time-and weather-worn semi-circle of red bricks that created the arch above her, drawing his attention to the creamy curve of her neck. His own neck prickled beneath his cashmere scarf as a surge of heat engulfed him and he wondered how it would feel to trace a finger down that smooth column to the soft spot at the base of her throat—
'This the place?'
The removalist's gruff voice caught Cam's attention. He nodded at the two men who'd appeared beside him, digging out the building's keys as he climbed the steps. 'Apartment six.'
At his approach, Didi's gaze darted to his. Wariness changed to recognition, then her brow puckered and her pretty lips twisted into something resembling a sneer. 'Well, if it isn't the man himself.' She pushed up, scattering crumbs. 'What the hell is going on?'
He stopped a few steps away. 'My sentiments

exactly, Miss O'Flanagan. I've been trying to contact you for the past two weeks.'

'Why?' Her eyes narrowed. 'I had a personal emergency to take care of.'

'And now you have another. I've been forced to call in the removalists.' He kept his tone civil, firm. 'If you can't give me an alternative address you leave me no choice but to have your belongings placed in storage.'

She blinked. '*Storage?* I've got another week.'

'No, Miss O'Flanagan, you do not. Which you'd know if you'd bothered to answer your phone.'

Her chin came up. 'The phone I *didn't* give you the number for.'

'There's always a way.'

She stiffened. 'Yes, I'm sure there is for someone like you. As it happens I don't have my phone at the moment.' The derision in her gaze fled as it shifted to the two men beside him, then to the truck parked at the kerb. 'I need more time. I have no job, thanks to that night—how am I going to rent an apartment?'

He shook his head. 'Reconstruction starts tomorrow morning.'

'*Tomorrow morning?* Well, that's just peachy.'

Her mouth pouted in a way that made him want to lick the fruity word right off her lips.

He quashed the urge and resultant heat immediately. Damn. Rather than her own lack of action, she made it sound as if *he* were the party responsible for her situation. Guilt niggled at him. She *had* shielded him from personal embarrassment, at least initially, by removing that poster. And he was her landlord after all.

'You can't put my things in storage,' she stated, a hint of nerves behind the grit. 'I *need* them.'

'So, you'll give me an address.'

'I told you, I don't have one.'

'You don't have a friend you can stay with?'

'I've only been in Melbourne a couple of months, so no.'

'You've obviously been staying with *someone* the past couple of weeks.' He didn't care for the image that unfurled in his mind—her compact body entwined with—

'Not in Melbourne—not that it's any of your business. *And as I've already told you, I had another week!*' Her blade-sharp voice sliced the exhaust-heavy air.

'No. You didn't.'

'I rang the agent last month about a week's extension and was told it was okay. As the landlord you're accountable for this mess.'

'Obviously there's been some sort of miscommunication.' He frowned as he stepped past her, unlocked the door and motioned to the waiting removalists. 'No extension would have been granted.'

'But it was.'

Grabbing her bag and box, she squeezed ahead of him into the narrow passage. He allowed her the dignity of opening her own front door with her key and followed her inside. She'd made some attempt at packing, he noted, glancing at the boxes stacked in the centre of the tiny living space. The odour of sour milk wafted from a carton on the kitchen sink. Perhaps she really had had an emergency.

She set the stuff she carried on the floor and marched to the fridge. 'There.' She gestured to the calendar, silver eyes sharp as knives, aimed at him. She'd written *Eviction Day* in bold red letters that dripped blood beneath it. On the wrong date.

Did she get things wrong on a regular basis? he wondered. She certainly had a knack for getting herself into trouble of one kind or another. But she was right about one thing; no matter whom

she'd spoken to at the rental agency, as her landlord, Cam was ultimately accountable.

'Look, why don't we have a coffee and let the
guys do their job?' he suggested, hoping to smooth
things along. 'Perhaps we can work something
out.'

'I'm not letting them out of my sight.' She glared
at the removalists loitering uncertainly in the
doorway.

'Start with the furniture,' Cam suggested to the
men. 'We'll sort out the rest in a while.' Then to
Didi, 'Pack what you need for now. Why don't you
try your workmates? Perhaps they can put you up
for a couple of days while we look for something
suitable.'

She flashed him a look that damn near froze
him to the spot, then grabbed her bag and box,
disappeared into the bedroom and shut the door.
He watched the men take the dilapidated furniture—what little there was of it—while he made
a call delaying his planned dinner meeting.

Five minutes later she reappeared. 'I've tried
my workmates. One's quit and gone interstate,
one's living with an aunt in a one-bedroom apartment, the other lives in a hostel. I've got stuff
here I can't—won't—put in storage. It's simply

too precious.' She bit her lip, looking perilously close to tears.

'Okay. Put it aside. I'll have it delivered to my apartment, it'll be safe there.'

She stared grimly at him. 'Not a chance.'

'For God's sake, be reasonable.' He could tell she was fiercely independent. Judging by the fact that she'd torn down the poster and spoken out for her fellow evictees he also knew she was a woman with scruples. 'We'll find you a place for the night. Leave it to me.'

She blew out a breath. 'Okay. But I'll be looking for you if any of my stuff goes missing.'

It took forty minutes longer to clear out the apartment but finally the van was gone, the items to be delivered to Cam's apartment clearly labelled. He waited until she'd exited, then locked up the building.

He turned at the bottom of the steps when he realised she wasn't following. She stood beneath the awning with her cardboard box and carry bag beside her. Her shoulders drooped and her body seemed to shrink inside the worn coat she wore, which may have been a fashion statement in the eighties but now looked sadly outdated.

He fought the ridiculous urge to bound up the

steps and gather her into his arms. The same urge
he used to get when his little sister came home at
dawn high on whatever her drug of choice was
that particular night.

'Let's go. What are you waiting for?' When she
didn't move he stifled an impatient breath—Amy
hadn't wanted his support either. 'You can't stay
here.'

Her eyes flashed with defiance. 'You have a
better suggestion?'

You could sleep in my bed. The associating
image smoked through his brain. Her spiky hair
tickling his nose as she stretched out on top of
him, eyes closed in pleasure. Fingers intertwined
and above his head, breasts to chest, thigh to
thigh...

He wasn't sure how, but he had the feeling she
knew exactly where his wayward thoughts were
going. He spoke stiffly through a clenched jaw.
'I'll book you a room for the evening until we
work something out tomorrow.'

Her response was an instant, 'No.'

'Didi, it's too late to do anything else tonight—'

'I mean...I can't go to a hotel.'

'Why ever not?'

Her gaze dropped to a cardboard carton on the

step beside her. He'd not noticed earlier, but now it drew his attention because some sort of scratching noise emanated from within.

'I rescued a cat on the way here. I'd never get it past the desk, and I need a litter tray and some food.' Her eyes met his. 'And don't suggest I take him to a shelter because I won't do it.'

'You'd sit on this step all night because of a cat?'

'Yes.' Her mouth set in a determined line as she bent down, scooted the box closer. 'You may not have a heart, Cameron Black, but I'll safeguard this animal from harm if it's the last thing I do.'

'Which it could very well be.' He shook his head. 'Amazing.' *She* was amazing—amazingly naïve or amazingly foolhardy. Or both. He checked his watch. It left him with no option but to move matters along immediately if he wanted to keep his already delayed dinner appointment on the other side of the city. Without looking at her he backtracked, picked up her overstuffed canvas shopping bag.

Didi watched him close one large fist over the straps then scrambled up. 'Hang about—where are you going with that?'

'My apartment.'

'No.' She made a grab for the bag but he'd already started down the steps.

She did *not* want to accompany Don't-Date-This-Man to his bachelor apartment. Wherever that might be. Where he ate breakfast or lounged semi-naked in front of sports TV. She did not want to know—her pulse skipped a beat in panic—whether he slept alone. She wanted nothing to do with his living arrangements or his lifestyle...or his crazy women. 'Stop!'

His stride barely faltered. 'You're coming home with me and I don't have time to argue about it.'

Home with him? She knew next to nothing about him—except how he made her insides roll about as if they'd become detached. 'I can't...' She caught up with him on the bottom step and tugged. Hard. One of the straps ripped away with a loud shirring sound, tipping the bag and spilling a few articles of intimate clothing onto the wet pavement. Water immediately soaked into the garments. 'Now look what you made me do.'

She regretted her slip the moment it left her mouth. His gaze landed on a lolly-pink thong centimetres from his shiny black shoes. Her *old* thong with the fraying elastic and the words 'Tempt me' faded by washing but still way too visible.

Oh, no. She dropped to her haunches, her fingers scrabbling on the wet pavement.

Too late.

Heat prickled her neck as she rose. The minuscule garment swung from one long finger. If she'd met his eyes she might have seen humour there but, frankly, right now he didn't seem the type and she wasn't risking it. She muttered a word she almost never used beneath her breath, careful to avoid skin contact as she snatched it from him.

She scooped the rest up, stuffing them back where they came from while rain splattered the pavement and her hair. Until Cameron shifted the umbrella so that it shielded her while leaving him exposed to the weather. 'It's all your fault,' she bit out.

'Am I to be held responsible for all your misfortunes, Didi?'

She straightened quickly, her eyes skidding straight into his with the inevitability of a train wreck. 'My life's been a disaster since the night I met you.' And even though she knew it was ridiculous, 'So, yes, I'm holding you responsible.'

His midnight-blue gaze didn't alter but a muscle twitched beneath his right eye. 'Makes one wonder what'll happen next. Maybe you should give up now—your misfortunes have a recurring habit of rubbing off on me.'

'I'm not rubbing anything off on you, Mr Black, you're managing your own rubbing very well.' Unfortunate choice of words. She forced herself to hold his gaze, which seemed to darken as they glared at each other.

Moisture sheened his face and raindrops lay like diamonds on the shoulders and collar of his very expensive wool coat. She knew it was wool because she could smell its distinctive scent chafing comfortably with his very expensive cologne. No, a man like him wouldn't tolerate something as inconvenient as another's misfortune.

'Maybe we could trade places some time,' she shot at him. But as she tripped up the steps again she had to admit he was offering her a generous and possibly very *in*convenient solution—for both of them. Or had she misunderstood? She picked up the cat's box, hefted its wobbling weight under one arm. 'Okay, so what exactly are you suggesting here, so I don't misunderstand?'

'You don't have a place to stay—and I'll take responsibility for that—so my apartment's a logical choice.'

'With my friend here? I'm not going anywhere without him.'

He glanced at the cat box, frowned. 'I guess it's settled, then. Tomorrow you can look for somewhere more suitable.'

She blew out a sigh, her breath fogging the air in front of her. Realistically, what alternative did she have? His offer was only for one night. A bed, somewhere safe...

She made the mistake of looking up at him again. At the dark eyes and sensual mouth—right now it was firm and inflexible. And absolutely captivating. How would it feel to be captivated by such a mouth? She drew a deep breath of chill night air. *Safe?*

'Tonight, then. Thank you.' She tried to keep her voice a notch above a croak. 'I'll need to stop at a pet shop for supplies on the way.'

He nodded, retrieving her one-handled bag, tucking it beneath one arm. She followed, dodging traffic and a tram as he headed towards a shiny late-model vehicle on the other side of the street while he fired rapid instructions into his mobile regarding the delivery of her stuff to the security guy at his apartment building.

The next experience was sitting beside him in

his big classy car that suddenly didn't feel so big. Soft leather seats, the lingering fragrance of aftershave and mints. Body heat.

She shrank against the door as far away as she could get and concentrated on the box on her knee, soothing the more and more agitated animal within with quiet murmurs. In the absence of radio or CD noise he sounded more like his larger jungle cousins. At least it gave her something else to focus on.

Until that familiar hand with its sprinkling of dark hair appeared in front of her as he leaned sideways to adjust an air vent on the dash sending a spurt of warm air her way. She held her breath. As if she needed any more warmth.

'So…this friend you've been with…' Checking the rear mirror, he replaced his hand on the steering wheel. 'That's not an option for a few days, I take it?'

'Accommodation-wise?' she said, keeping her tone enigmatic. 'Marysville's a long drive away. My working life's here, in Melbourne.' When she found another job, that was.

She had something to prove. To her family, to herself. It didn't help that she'd told them she'd found work in a gallery and had a stunning apartment overlooking the Yarra. When she'd returned from a couple of years overseas after leaving school, they'd told her if she didn't intend going to university or making some sort of commitment and/or compromise she was on her own. She'd taken them literally and moved out.

They saw her passion for textile design as a waste of time—an argument she was never going to win. Creativity didn't pay; artists didn't make money. And until she did, until she showed them what she was capable of, she was stuck with wait-ressing—or not, since she was now unemployed.

They stopped at a small supermarket for pet supplies, and fifteen minutes later she followed his broad-shouldered shape through the revolving glass door of a luxury building.

Then he was whisking her skywards to his apartment. His penthouse apartment. But as she stepped into the living room surprise knocked her back a step. She hadn't expected to find his taste so...formal, so cool. So impersonal.

Maybe she should have.

Still holding the cat's box, she took in her surroundings. Almost everything was white. Stark white sofas bordered a black rug over white mar-bled floor tiles that seemed to go on for ever, giving an impression of endless space. A couple of glass-topped occasional tables with black-shaded lamps that threw out a harsh bleached light. Oyster-coloured curtains framed night-darkened floor-to-ceiling windows, which offered a stunning view of Melbourne's high rises.

Not a speck of dust, she noted as her eyes scanned the room. Nothing out of place. Not a coffee cup, TV guide, or book in sight. Nothing to make it homey or liveable. How did anyone live in such sparse surroundings? Because he probably spent little time here, she decided. Probably busy sleeping elsewhere.

She wandered to the window. 'Great view from up here. I imagine you see some beautiful sunsets—if you take the time to look.'

'Sunrise actually.' He set her bag on the floor. 'The view faces east. And yes, I make the time.'

'I didn't take you for the contemplative sort.'

'You wouldn't, would you? You're the sort who makes snap decisions about people before you have the facts. You're also impulsive and driven by emotions. You only see what you want to see.'

His blunt appraisal stung. Some sort of comeback was due and she lifted her chin. 'Whereas you're driven by cool, calculating intellect.' More like sunrise was a pretty backdrop while he planned how to make his next million. 'Sunrise should be about a new day—hope—something that comes from the heart… Oh, my…'

She trailed off as her gaze snagged on a major piece of textile art that hadn't been visible from the entrance. Without taking her eyes from it, she fished in her bag for her rose-tinted reading glasses and moved in for a closer inspection.

The asymmetric mural took up almost the entire wall, a forest bound with thread and paint beneath swirling drifts of snowflakes constructed with silver thread and beads in a disordered hexagonal fashion. She couldn't resist reaching out to touch the tactile feast, the subtly different shades of texture. 'A Sheila Dodd original. It must be worth a fortune.'

'Yes, and yes. You're familiar with her work?' His tone turned considering, as if he didn't believe someone like Didi would know anything about artists like Sheila Dodd. Or Monet for that matter.

She met his speculative gaze full-on. 'She's my inspiration.'

'Inspiration… For what exactly?'

'What I do.' Didi turned back to admire the work but didn't elaborate on the fact that she produced pieces along similar lines to the prominent Aussie artist and hoped to one day bathe in the same limelight. 'I enjoy creating things, whether it's food or fashion or fabric.' She flicked him a glance. 'That surprises you.'

'I'm fast learning not to be surprised by anything about you.'

He was watching her with an expression she either couldn't or didn't want to read. All she knew was it made her...prickly, itchy. Bitchy. 'It's a pity it's all so—' she waved her free hand at the room '—monochrome.'

One eyebrow rose. 'My designer thought otherwise.' Then he seemed to reflect on that a moment and said, 'What would you change?' as if he'd never given his choice of interior decoration a thought.

'Personal opinion of course, but you don't think it's lacking a little warmth and intimacy?' When he didn't reply she looked around at the bare surfaces. 'Where's the ambience? A few homey pieces like photos, a rock collection, a pottery figurine. A mix of plump red or apricot cushions, warm yellow light and a bluesy CD.'

Typical Didi-speak, but now the warmth and intimacy thing seemed to take hold as he continued to watch her. To distract herself she set her box on the floor, withdrew Charlie, buried her face in his soft fur and changed the topic. 'Hey, you're safe now, little guy.' *But was she?*

'It suits me the way it is.' He turned his attention to Charlie. 'That cat looks remarkably healthy for a stray. Are you sure it was abandoned?'

She rubbed the round tight tummy. 'True, but if you found a cat stuffed in a box tied up with string and left by a toilet block what would you assume?'

He nodded, straightened, all formal again. 'The bedroom's this way.' His tone matched his choice of furnishings—minimalist. 'It has an enclosed balcony. Please keep the cat confined to that area.'

She followed him down a wide corridor. As she passed she glimpsed what must be his bedroom, then another filled with gym equipment...and her stuff.

'Davis, the security guy downstairs, had your gear put in here.' He gestured towards it, then stopped at the third door, swung it open. The mountain of cream and gold quilt looked inviting on the big double bed. 'The guest bathroom's at the end of the corridor.'

'Great,' she said into the tense silence. Her initial snap judgement might have been premature. How many people would have put themselves out this way for a virtual stranger? She murmured, 'Thank you.'

He nodded, checked his watch. 'I'm unlikely to be back before midnight so make yourself at home. If you're hungry, feel free to fix something to eat.'

'Thanks.' Her gaze turned back to the bedroom. To the bed covered in *his* sheets. A shaft of heat slid through her belly. 'Um…thanks again, I'll be fine. Goodnight,' she managed, and stepped inside. Closed the door.

She waited till she heard his footsteps fade. 'Well, Charlie…' She smoothed his fur and set him down. 'So I guess it's tuna fish dinner for you and a hot bath for me.' But even though she forced herself to keep thoughts and self-talk upbeat she wondered with an ever-increasing knot in her stomach what she'd got herself into.

CHAPTER THREE

CAM glanced at the time on his computer screen as he checked his last unread email. Half past midnight. Surely his house-guest would be asleep by now? Because he didn't want to have to deal with her again tonight he'd stopped by his office on his way home from dinner.

Nor did he want to dwell on the fact that for some perverse reason she'd been slipping into his dreams over the past couple of weeks and doing wicked things to his libido. Of course she'd been on his mind, he told himself—she'd caused him unnecessary inconvenience and concern.

He switched off his computer, swiped his hands over the back of his neck. Okay, dreams—he could deal with those—but in-the-flesh reality was a different matter. So he'd give her another half-hour to be on the safe side.

But that didn't stop him from imagining her in his apartment. Relaxing in the bathroom's spa and steaming it up with her intriguing blend of feminine fragrance. Drinking from his cups. Curled between his sheets with only one room separating them.

He made a coffee in the kitchenette, then sat at his secretary's desk and flicked through *The Age* to kill time and divert his thoughts from what was going on in his apartment.

But his mind refused to glance further than the latest headlines. Would Didi remember his instructions to keep the no doubt flea-infested cat in her room, preferably on the balcony? Had she even heard them? he wondered, then shook his head. He had a feeling she wasn't good at following instructions.

She'd not yet shared with him the information that she'd lost her job. Perhaps she had something else lined up already, but he seriously doubted it. Because Didi O'Flanagan seemed to be a woman who danced to her own tune, when and wherever it suited her.

Irresponsible? He blew on his coffee. He'd reserve judgement on that. But he *was* surprised she recognised his Sheila Dodd.

Was that a tad pretentious of him?

He flicked through the pages with disinterest until his gaze snagged on a photo of his ex and thoughts of Didi fled as his fingers tightened on the paper. Katrina. On the arm of Melbourne's latest most eligible bachelor—soon to be ex-bachelor judging by the size of that rock on Kat's finger. The coffee turned bitter on his tongue. Unlike Cam, Jacob Beaumont Junior was from old money. His father owned half a shipping fleet and an airline—the perfect pedigree required for a suitable match for the daughter of an influential MP on his way to Australia's top job.

His harsh jeer echoed around the empty room. He'd thought Katrina the perfect woman. Tall, dark-haired, educated, meticulously groomed. Unashamedly uninhibited in the bedroom, the perfect conversationalist whatever company they surrounded themselves with, as driven to succeed as he was.

Until he'd revealed his background.

Her demolition of their relationship had been swift and vehement. In her eyes his family's history defined who *he* was—and consigned him to the lowest form of life. It didn't matter that he'd clawed his way out of the gutter, and had constructed a life he could take pride in. That he was stronger for past experiences, wiser, more perceptive of others' needs and motivation.

The page came away from the rest of the paper as he crumpled it in his fist, then tossed it in the bin. Her betrayal had severed an artery. Aristocrats were never going to let him into their world, no matter how successful he was now.

He liked women. He enjoyed their company. He liked the way they smelled, the feel of feminine softness against his body. But laying his heart on the line again was not going to happen. From now on he'd trust no one with his past. He didn't intend to remain celibate for the rest of his life, but from this day forward there'd be no emotional entanglements.

Cam let himself in with careful stealth so as not to awaken his sleeping guest. He didn't notice her at first. He just assumed she'd left every light in the apartment on because she had no idea about energy conservation. Annoyance prickled at him as he strode to the kitchen and flicked off the switch.

He was about to turn off the living-room lamp when he saw her. Rather, he saw her pyjama-clad backside—poking out from behind his white leather sofa. Red and green tartan flannelette.

He remained perfectly still while every male cell in his body jerked to attention. From where he stood he could see the soles of her feet and a band of creamy skin above the pyjama's waistband. What the hell was she up to?

Then he heard her croon softly, her voice muffled by the sofa, and watched, immobile, blood pooling in his groin as the compact little bottom wiggled and began backing out, her movements inevitably tugging the elastic lower...

'Problem?'

The wiggling stopped, then resumed at a frantic pace accompanied by a hiss, then the disconcerting sound of fabric tearing. 'Ouch!'

Didi appeared clutching an angry armful of spiked fur, damp blonde hair in similar disarray, her eyes huge, too huge for her elfin face, reminding him again of that pixie.

'I didn't hear you,' she said with a breathy catch to her voice that made him think of hot nights, hotter bodies.

'Obviously.'

'Charlie escaped. Um...there's a tiny claw hole—a couple actually...in the back of your sofa.' She closed her teeth over her bottom lip, then smiled up at him. 'Lucky for us they're not where you can see them, isn't it?'

The way she did that...artfully innocent or

cunningly cute? He shook his head. 'Lucky for Charlie.'

Her smile dimmed. Snuggling the creature against her, she rose. 'If you have a pair of nail trimmers handy, I'll fix these claws right now.'

The shapeless flannelette swamped her. It should have been a blessing but it had the opposite effect. A sliver of protectiveness—or lust—snaked through his veins and coiled low in his body.

It had to be lust.

He crossed to the window, stood with his back to her to hide his body's response. 'Just take yourself and that damn cat back to bed and shut the door behind you.' *And stay there.*

'You don't like animals. How sad.'

The quiet censure in her tone put him on the defensive. 'I don't like animals *in my apartment.*'

'That's why I'd never live in an apartment. No garden, no fresh air and sky, no pets.'

He tried to confine his gaze to his own reflection in the night-darkened glass, but like lightning to metal his eyes were drawn to the image of the woman behind him. To the way her delicate fingers massaged the cat's fur. To the way her pyjama top dipped on one side exposing a sharply delineated collarbone—

'So you'll be wanting to find yourself somewhere more to your liking as soon as possible.'

The air stirred with a tense silence that echoed around his heart. Pulled at him as he heard her say, 'Naturally,' and watched her reflection turn and walk away, shoulders slumped. His fingers curled and tightened at his sides. Damn it.

Why had he taken his hostility towards Kat out on his house-guest? Even if she did rub him the wrong way. In so many ways... Shaking unwanted feelings off, he followed her ribbon of freshly showered almonds-and-honey scent along the hall. 'Didi...'

She halted at her door, hugging her cat to her like a child with a teddy bear. But she gave him no time to form the words he might have said. 'Thank you for your generosity this evening, Cameron Black. Goodnight.'

The door closed with a tight click, leaving only her fragrance to mingle with his self-recrimination.

He stared at the barrier a moment, listening to the sound of her moving around on the other side and wondering what she was doing. When the sound stopped abruptly, he couldn't help but picture her climbing into bed in those oversized pyjamas.

A big picture, a bad picture. A very bad picture because he didn't want to think about what those pyjamas hid. Nor did he want to imagine how he might go about finding out once and for all what that mobile mouth of hers tasted like, even if it was just to shut her up for a moment or two.

He gulped in a deep breath, heard it whistle out through his teeth. Finally he peeled his gaze away from the paintwork. Right now was a good time to hit the treadmill running.

The sound of his mobile woke Cameron from a sleep crowded with unwanted dreams of passionate pixies. Eyes still closed, he reached for the phone. 'Cameron Black.'

'Good morning, Mr Black. Sasha Needham calling for Sheila Dodd. I apologise for ringing you this early but I've just had a call from Sheila in the UK.'

'Yes?' Cam dragged his eyes open, checked the digital clock on his night stand. Five forty-five a.m.

'Sheila sends her sincere apologies but she's unable to finish the piece you commissioned within the agreed time frame. She's had a family crisis and will be staying on in the UK for the next few weeks.'

He pushed upright, wide awake now and already one step ahead. 'The gallery opens in less than three weeks.'

'I'm so sorry, Mr Black. Sheila realises it's short notice. She's given me the names of some possible alternatives…'

He closed his eyes again, scrubbed a hand over his morning stubble. 'Email them to me along with their credentials et cetera and I'll get back to you.'

Tossing off the quilt, he rose quickly, his bare feet barely registering the change from plush carpet to cool tiles as he moved to the bathroom and splashed cold water over his face.

Over the past two years he'd worked like a demon to turn a graffiti-covered warehouse in Melbourne's inner suburbs into something unique. An art gallery, not only for prominent artists but also for undiscovered talent from the lower socioeconomic areas. An opportunity for those willing to put in the effort to start something worthwhile. A second chance.

The way he'd been given a second chance.

He stared into his own eyes. Heaven knew where he'd be now without it. He'd been one of those kids, and this gallery was a memorial to the one person who'd made it possible to start over.

Cam had poured a large sum of money into publicity; the minister for the arts was attending the official opening along with the press. If he couldn't have Sheila's work on display in time for the opening, he'd damn well have to find someone else pronto.

Twenty minutes later, showered and dressed, Cam slid open the French doors and welcomed the sounds of distant early morning traffic and brisk winter wind blowing through the potted palms on his sky garden patio. The fading glow of sunrise tinged the clouds a dirty pink, crisp air tingled his cheeks. He shrugged inside his suit jacket. Who said apartment living and nature were mutually exclusive?

Didi O'Flanagan.

Her image exploded into his mind and he pinched the bridge of his nose. As if he hadn't seen enough of her in his dreams last night; reclining on his desk, wearing nothing but those damn pink glasses and munching on red apples, for heaven's sake. He shook it away. He should have arranged a time to meet this morning to discuss further arrangements. If he wasn't careful she could end up here for God knew how long.

Right now he had a more urgent problem. Slurping strong black coffee, he checked his mobile for the names Sheila's assistant had promised to send. Nothing yet.

'Wow!'

He turned at the sound of Didi's voice, mighty relieved when she appeared wearing a cover-all pink dressing gown. 'Good morning.' His relief was short-lived—she smiled at him as she bit into a shiny red apple.

'Good morning.' Silver eyes sparkling, she waved the thing in the air like a damn trophy, indicating their surroundings. 'This garden's amazing! Is that a kumquat tree?' she said, barely drawing breath and moving to his tubbed specimen laden with tiny orange fruit. 'I just love kumquat marmalade.'

'Ah, we need to discuss—'

His mobile cut the rest of his sentence off. Didi studied him as he took the call. Impeccably dressed in dark suit, wrinkle-free white shirt and a tie the colour of blueberries. His cedar-wood fragrance wafting on the air, the broad shape of his shoulders, the sexy strip of neck between his jacket and newly cut hair as he turned and began walking inside. Heat shivered through her and lodged low in her belly. Tall, dark, gorgeous.

Forget gorgeous.

Yep, she seriously needed to forget gorgeous. Cameron Black was the reason she no longer had an apartment. And because of her outburst at that function a fortnight ago, *thanks to him,* she needed to look for another job, which left her no time to work on the important things like establishing her career as an artist.

If she could just win that chance…

To give him privacy while he took his call, she chomped on the apple she'd helped herself to in the kitchen and admired the view a few moments, then rescued his coffee and carried it inside.

She found him studying his laptop at the dining-room table, brow furrowed, mouth pursed in a seriously sexy way, and for an insane moment she wondered how he'd react if she walked over there and pressed her lips against his.

Bad thought. This man was so not her type. This man was the type of successful entrepreneur her parents would approve of, which made him *all wrong.*

So she had to ask, 'What, no destitute families to evict today?' as she set his coffee cup on the table beside him.

He didn't look up; his only reply was, 'Humph.'

Had he even heard her? Then she made the mistake of looking at his eyes. Framed by ridiculously long lashes, they were the colour of his tie—dark blueberry—and the clouds in them had her softening despite herself. 'Anything I can do?'

Fingers tense on the table, he leaned back against the chair, his suit jacket falling open and giving her a view of broad chest, his dark nipples barely visible beneath the white shirt. 'Not unless you know someone with Sheila Dodd's expertise who can whip up something remarkable at short notice.'

Processing his words, she dragged her gaze away from his superhero body. 'Why?' she queried carefully.

'I'm opening a gallery in less than three weeks. The press will be there, along with a host of art critics, and I need something spectacular for the main wall. I commissioned Sheila but she's overseas dealing with some sort of family crisis.' His breath steamed out through his nostrils and he smacked the table with a hefty palm. 'Damn it!'

'So you want someone similarly experienced with textiles.' Dared she mention Didi O'Flanagan's considerably *less* experienced expertise?

He scrubbed his hands over his cheeks, a wholly masculine sound—the only sound in the quiet room apart from the thump of Didi's heart galloping in nervous anticipation.

'Right now I'd settle for anything, bar tomboy stitch or macramé.'

'Hmm.' She drew in a tentative breath. 'Leave it with me. I'll have something for you to look at by tonight.'

His hands paused on his jaw and Didi found those unnerving blueberry eyes focused on her. 'You know someone?' Spoken with barely concealed incredulity.

'Yes.' *Surprising as that might seem to you. And just wait till you find out who.*

'Who?' he demanded.

She shook her head. 'No questions.' Her mouth turned dry. Could she impress this guy enough to display her work? 'You're going to the office, right?' A horrible thought occurred to her. 'You *do* have an office somewhere, don't you?' Preferably a long way away.

'I do.' But as he lowered his hands to the table top she couldn't help but note the inflexible set of his jaw and his eyes didn't precisely brim with confidence.

'Look, I know we didn't exactly hit it off, and last night…well, all is forgiven if—'

'*You're* forgiving *me?*' His brows rose. 'By the way, how's that cat this morning? More to the point, *where is* that cat this morning?'

Didi huffed out a breath, knowing she'd made a wrong turn somewhere. 'Charlie's fine, sleeping on my pyjamas last time I looked.' She waved a hand as if it could erase last night's little foray behind the sofa. 'Forget about that for now.' *Please.* 'Do you trust me in your apartment?'

His shoulders lifted inside his jacket, then he seemed to relax momentarily and a corner of his mouth kicked up. 'What's the worst that can happen?'

Several scenarios presented themselves, none of which Didi wanted to contemplate. She forced a smile back at him. 'You give macramé a go?'

Didi waited fifteen minutes just in case Cameron changed his mind and came back. The phone rang and she had a moment when she thought he might have changed his mind, but it must have been a wrong number because whoever it was hung up. Thoughtful, she stared at the handset as she replaced it on its base. Was it him checking in with last-minute instructions? Or was he checking that she hadn't run off with his valuables? Or perhaps it was a lady friend who'd hung up at the sound of a female voice?

She shrugged away the odd little niggle that thought provoked, then hurried to where her boxes of supplies had been stashed, dragged them out and got busy. She unearthed her portfolio with photographs of smaller pieces she'd either sold or still had in her boxes. She had no idea what he wanted for the gallery, but first she had to impress him with her work.

She had several pieces in various stages of completion, but her pride and joy was a quilt-sized work stretched on a frame, covered in black plastic and taped for safety. And how serendipitous that it blended so well with his living room, she thought, unwrapping it. Similar to Sheila's work with black, white and silver and various shades between, but Didi had used fire-engine red as a focal colour.

She set the piece against a bare wall, stood back and cast a critical eye over it.

Twigs she'd painstakingly collected and bound in black, white and silver thread made up the tree, the leaves silver filigree she'd constructed by hand at a jewellery class. An embroidered black serpent wound its way through the branches along a piece of old barbed wire. Just visible behind the action were the subtly spray-painted but unmistakeably erotic shapes of male and female. The apples of red silk layered with organza, thread and delicately spray-painted for a three-dimensional effect completed the picture.

She'd never shown her family. It would hurt too much to hear their dismissal of something she'd put her heart and soul into for months, using any spare cash she earned to purchase the supplies she needed.

The big question was would it be good enough to convince Cameron Black to take a chance on her?

He arrived home late. Didi had spent the day working on new material and suddenly there he was, watching her from across the living room with a doubtful expression in his eyes. Of course,

he would, wouldn't he? With every square cen-
timetre of his ever-so-clean table covered in her
stuff.

'Hi.' She threaded her needle through a piece of
fabric, took off her glasses, blinking up at him as
her eyes adjusted. 'I'm sorry about the mess—I'll
clean it up right this—'

'Forget the mess. I don't have time to waste. I've
got less than three weeks.' Crossing the room, he
shrugged off his jacket, slung it on the back of
a dining-room chair at the far end of the table.
Didi couldn't help but notice Mr Immaculate's
shirt looked as pristine as it had when he'd left
this morning.

His eyes took in her scraps of fabric and silks
then flicked to the sheet-draped work against the
wall, back to her. Comprehension dawned. 'So,
you're the artist.' He sounded disappointed.

Her pulse took a leap. Squashing down her insecurities, she replied, 'I hope so.'

'That's why you recognised Sheila's work.'

She nodded. 'I've always loved textiles. I took
one of her workshops in Sydney a few years ago.'

He crossed his arms over his chest. 'So…what
do you have to show me?'

A hiatus while she stopped breathing. Oh,

cripes, she wished he hadn't said it in quite that way with quite that expression in his eyes. Scepticism. Her art was the one thing that truly mattered to her.

Somehow she managed to make it across the room. Her arm trembled as she withdrew the sheet. And waited for a response. Any response.

The right response.

She thought she heard him mutter, 'Apples again,' and saw his jaw tighten.

He had something against apples? 'It's called Before the Temptation.'

'What else could you call it?' His wry response still gave her no clue to his thoughts.

Almost unbearable. How long he studied it, immobile, feet spread and arms crossed, she couldn't be sure. Seconds? Minutes? She counted the beats of her heart. Lost count.

Finally, he nodded. 'Okay, Didi, you've got yourself a commission. Two and a half weeks to come up with something of the same standard.'

Relief and excitement sent her soaring on helium balloons, making her voice breathless when she said, 'I'll need to know what you have in mind.'

'Something half as big again. The rest's up to you. I want your best.'

'You'll have it.'

'Don't let me down,' he continued. 'The press will be there, the minister for arts. I can't afford—'

'I won't let you down.'

He nodded. 'I'm not an artist, but I'm guessing it'll take all your time with only two and a half weeks to completion. All day, possibly some evening work too. Have you considered that?'

She nodded. 'Not a problem. I no longer work for the catering company, so I'm all yours.'

Hands dipping into trouser pockets, his gaze swung to her at last, and she was blasted by the full force of those eyes—not sceptical now, but... unreadable in the room's cool electric lights. They darkened considerably as his gaze flicked down over her tight black T-shirt and apricot chiffon scarf around her waist, to the black leggings and bare feet.

Oh... Her toes curled against the smooth tiles, her fingers slid down the front of her thighs as her heart did a strange tumble. Why the heck did her body react to him the way it did? As if he could draw her into those bottomless pools and— No. She'd let herself be drawn into a man's eyes once, and that had been one time too many. Jay had captivated her from the start, the way he had so many women. It was because of him she'd never trust a man's looks again, nor the way he might make her feel.

Because whatever her feelings might be towards a man, she couldn't trust him to reciprocate. Even when his eyes told her otherwise. She could only nod before clearing her throat. 'I—'

'You'll need space to work.'

'Yes.' No. Her balloons deflated. She didn't *have* space.

'So you'll remain here until the work's completed.' Blunt, a rusty knife on sandstone.

No time to reply.

He swivelled away, back bristling with tension, and headed towards the kitchen. 'Less than three weeks, Didi. You've got yourself a chance— use it.'

CHAPTER FOUR

DIDI heard the sound of the fridge door open, something hit the kitchen bench with a thwack, and realised she'd eaten nothing since that apple at breakfast. Nor could she now with her stomach twisted into hard, indigestible knots.

Work *here?* In this man's apartment? The man who ostensibly didn't give a fig for the less fortunate yet took in a stranger with a cat, no questions asked...well, almost none.

He wasn't the man she'd first assumed, she had to admit. And he was giving her the chance of a lifetime.

To anchor herself she clutched the front of her T-shirt while she replayed the last few moments. She'd wanted, more than she'd ever wanted anything, him to give her the commission, she just hadn't thought beyond that happy moment to the day-to-day/day-to-*night* practicalities.

Several long days. And nights.

Cam hadn't even bothered to comment on her

work. The first person she'd exposed her best piece to, laying her vulnerability on the line, and not a single comment apart from a rude 'apples again'—what was that all about? Typical of the wealthy, she thought with an inward sneer. It reminded her of her family's dismissive attitude towards her art.

And yet...he had an original Sheila Dodd on his wall and he was opening a gallery, which had to mean he valued art. She thought of his eyes, the pulse-accelerating way he'd looked at her... Perhaps there was another reason he'd stalked off as if the demons from hell snapped at his heels...

She shook off the thought and all its complications—forget all that. This was her big chance, maybe her only chance to show what she was capable of.

Cam put two frozen gourmet meals in the microwave, set the timer, then leaned against the bench, uncomfortably aware that if Didi chose that moment to follow, she'd be in no doubt as to why he'd walked away before they'd formalised any kind of agreement.

For a moment he'd considered remaining in front of the open refrigerator door for a few moments. Cool the fires within. The woman was a sorceress in pixie clothing. How else could she have bewitched him so utterly? One glance and he knew for certain that underneath the figure-hugging black she was moulded just the way he'd dreamed. All she needed was the wings.

Hell.

And he'd just made an arrangement that required her here, in his apartment, for the next two and a half weeks. He shook his head at the irony.

No. This was strictly business. If she was going to be working in the dining/living room in the evenings—which was the ideal room with its floor-to-ceiling windows and huge table—wearing those figure-hugging outfits... He'd stay longer at the office and sleep on the futon. Maybe he should check into a hotel.

Then how would he keep an eye on her progress?

He needed to set some parameters, but some sort of celebratory offering was probably required first. A drink? He moved to the refrigerator once more, whipped out a bottle of Moët et Chandon Vintage Rosé, grabbed two glasses and headed to the living area.

Struck again by the sight of her sensational art

against the wall, he slowed to study it once more. Who'd have thought the somewhat crazy little waitress was so talented? It would look right at home in the best galleries in the country. It looked right at home in his living room.

So did Didi.

She stood facing the windows, her hands laced together behind her head. The down-lights spangled her contrived riot of hair and he could smell her sweet almond fragrance from the other side of the room. He did his best to ignore her relaxed pose against Melbourne's diamond-studded deep velvet panorama as she stretched her body from side to side, no doubt flexing her spine after hours of close work.

But there was something spellbinding about the way she moved, as if she listened to some inner rhythm, that had his feet stapled to the floor. His blood pounded thickly as his gaze devoured the slim waist and compact little ass like some ravenous beast. And those legs... How would they feel clamped around his waist?

Dangerous curves.

Dangerous thoughts.

'We haven't ironed out the details of this arrangement,' she said.

Her voice startled him out of his semi-dazed state. Using his trick and watching him in the glass. Their eyes met for a brief moment, then again when she turned to face him. It was in her gaze too—a mutual awareness, quickly banked. If he'd blinked he'd have missed it.

'No, we haven't.' He moved to the table, set down the bottle and glasses, dismissing the urge to suggest an alternative and completely inappropriate way to celebrate: *Sealed with a kiss.* Like a spark to oxygen, the thought of locking lips with Didi exploded into stunning, breathtaking life. He grappled with the bottle's foil and cork. With those full rosy lips she'd suck away any bargaining power he possessed, of that he had no doubt. And on that not-so-sobering note, he said, 'We'll drink to it first.'

Didi shook her head. As much as she loved champers—and this looked like a bottle of the very expensive variety—this was way too important. 'Details first. How much am I worth?'

He named a figure that swept the air out of her lungs with a whoosh.

'That's if you're finished within the time frame,' he reminded her.

She was suddenly elated and terrified all at

once. That amount was seriously serious. It would set her up for a long time. Show her family artists *did* make money and finally, maybe, they'd accept her choice. Accept her. How long had she craved their acceptance, their pride? Doubts crept in. Was she up for it? 'I'll need an advance to purchase supplies.'

'No problem. I can order you a credit card or give you cash, whichever you prefer. The apartment's at your disposal day and night.'

She nodded, trying to absorb the details. At least he'd be out during the day, but evenings... 'I'm not used to people watching me work—or looking at the unfinished product.'

'I'm paying you enough—that gives me the right to view it any time.'

He poured the bubbly into the glasses, looking satisfied with the deal. And why not? He dealt with mega bucks on a daily basis; this was probably no more than a drop in the Pacific Ocean to him. And he was correct—that amount of money on an unknown artist gave him every right to track her progress.

'I'll need time to design and collect materials.'

'Not too long. I want to see something tangible within a few days.'

Panic stations. 'Artists don't work like that.'

'Ah, but this one will. It's too important, for both of us.'

He held up a full glass, sparkling with pink liquid, his eyes focused on hers and she felt...respect? No one had ever afforded her work that compliment so she wasn't sure of her perceptions. She stood by the window too strung out with emotion to move. Or speak.

'Lost for words, Didi?' His voice held a hint of humour, deep and warm, and he walked towards her with both glasses. 'I have every confidence in you. Don't doubt yourself or your abilities.'

She drew herself up as he approached. 'I don't.'

'Good.'

'Even though *you* haven't said a word about my work,' she pointed out.

'Doesn't the fact that I'm commissioning you say it all?' His knuckles inevitably skimmed hers as he handed her the pink bubbly, sending a fizz of sensation through her fingers and up her arm. That first brief skin-to-skin contact left her wanting...more.

'We're in this together,' he said. 'A team. You create and I'll provide you with meals, coffee, chocolate, headache pills if necessary...whatever you need.'

She clinked her glass to his. 'Okay. To teamwork.' The fruity bubbles sparkled through her system as she took the first sip, their happy hiss and pop tickling her nose and prompting her to smile and say, 'I'll tell you now, I only eat dark chocolate. Soft centres.'

'Ah, a woman after my own taste.'

He grinned, an easy grin that reminded her of the first uncomplicated moment when she'd met him when he was just an attractive man with a flirtatious wit. Like Jay. Despite the warning bells that told her to avoid such men at all costs, she grinned right back. And why not? It wasn't as if they were going to fall into bed—she wouldn't let that happen. 'And olives,' she continued. 'You like olives, if my memory serves correctly.'

'Cheese and olive balls...' His smile faded and just like that the atmosphere changed from light and casual to something darker, deeper. Different.

His gaze dropped to her mouth, which suddenly felt dry and chapped and tingly and she had to force herself not to run her tongue over her lips.

Her relationship with Jay had tarnished the way she viewed men. But none had made her feel so aware of herself as a woman. And if she was right in her assumption of his reaction, a desirable woman. He could even—perhaps—polish that tarnish away.

If she moved closer would he kiss her?

She couldn't help it, she looked right back. She could imagine being kissed by those lips. Her own were practically puckering up in anticipation.

And where would that leave her?

In that big bad bed of his having the best sex of her life?

And more breathless and brainless than she already was, no doubt.

Big mistake. She knew next to nothing about him except that he was rich, gorgeous...and attracted to her. And his poster-boy status suggested a playboy and put her defences on alert. Yep, way too much like Jay.

So she chose the only alternative and stepped back. Away. Paying careful attention to keep her glass—and her voice—steady as she said, 'Tell me about this gallery of yours.'

He regarded her a moment through thoughtful eyes as if he, too, was mulling over the sexual tension between them. 'It's my latest building development.'

'Another bunch of displaced people, then?' And instantly felt less-than-stellar for the jibe. Did she want to blow this whole deal before she got started? Especially when his eyes glinted with some emotion she didn't recognise... Regret? For past business actions maybe? Or for something that struck much deeper and closer to the heart.

She was still frowning when he said, 'I'm not the bastard you seem to think I am.' And took a breath—

She perked up, ready to listen. Personal information, great, he hadn't volunteered a word about his personal life. But either the sound of scratching and an annoyed yowl from her bedroom distracted him or he deliberately chose not to elaborate.

'Charlie,' she murmured. 'He's lonely. And hungry, no doubt.'

'No doubt.' The dismissive tone didn't bode well for poor Charlie. 'It was a disused warehouse,' he continued, ignoring the feline sounds. 'Boarded up and covered in graffiti. High ceilings, plenty of space. It has a whole new look.'

'What type of art are you showcasing?'

'Paintings, textiles, jewellery, you name it. The idea is to foster new talent.'

'So why a Sheila Dodd commission? She's hardly new.'

'I've admired her work for several years and a big name brings in more customers and encourages new sales.'

'Why me? With your contacts you must know others who fit the bill.'

'This opening's being publicised as a big event in the art community. I don't have the time to look for someone at such short notice.' He glanced at the piece, looked back to her. 'Your work's unique—I'm prepared to take a chance. I want you.'

His voice was neutral, all business, but his eyes...his eyes imbued a different meaning to those last three words. Her pulse seemed to throb in her throat, making it difficult to swallow. She gulped down more wine and held his gaze.

But he didn't want her so much as *need* her and that gave her a sense of power that she'd never had. Which emboldened her to say, 'I have another request... Perhaps favour is a better word? It's about Charlie.'

'Ah. Yes. Charlie.' His tone predictably cooled.

'Could we perhaps compromise?' Her parents had often mentioned the word and Didi in the same breath. 'If I'm here for nearly three weeks, it's hardly fair to keep him shut away by himself all day while I work. Would you agree to him being in here with me?' Cameron didn't look impressed with her idea—his brows lowered, his lips thinned, then pursed as if about to speak. 'And I know he'd love the sky garden,' she hurried on. 'He couldn't do much damage there and if I could leave the door open a fraction...'

He blew out a sigh. 'I guess we can try it before he strips the paintwork on the bedroom door to kingdom come.'

She paused, knowing, hating that she had to say, 'I love him to bits, but I know I'm going to have trouble finding a place that will take me *and* a pet...if you know anyone who wants a cat...' She blinked away a sudden moisture.

'I'll ask around at the office,' he said. 'Meanwhile he's okay here.'

'Thank you.' She polished off her wine and felt the grin pull at her cheeks as the bubbly danced through her system. 'And it's a wonderful compromise. I'll go tell him the good news now.'

'You do that. Then we'll eat; I assume you're hungry?'

'Famished,' she called as she all but skipped on

those pretty bare feet across the room and disappeared from view down the passage. 'All I've had today is an apple.'

Yeah. The apple. Cameron stared at the place where she'd been seconds ago. It was as if she'd left something of herself there. Hell, his whole apartment suddenly seemed crammed with her presence. His gaze lobbed on the usually pristine dining-room table, now a jumble stall jammed with her stuff. Littering his floor was a haphazard scatter of cardboard boxes brimming with colour. A fresh spicy fragrance permeated the air.

It was as if a cellar had been opened to let in the sunshine.

He slammed the door on his overactive imagination. Shaking his head at the absurdity, he strode to the kitchen. What the hell was wrong with him? He despised clutter. Didn't tolerate disorganised people. The squalid mess of his childhood would live with him for the rest of his life.

Three weeks. For art's sake he could manage three weeks. And what was that about compromise? She obviously had no idea of the meaning of the word... What *was* that odour?

He glared at the two containers as he yanked them out of the microwave. One hot gourmet dinner and one ruined tray of greying prime fillet steak, steamed beyond redemption. Blast it.

'What's that smell?' Didi appeared at the door with the cat in her arms and wrinkling her nose.

'Charlie's dinner. What say we eat out? My treat.' He whisked the remaining gourmet plate to the back of the bench then, grabbing a knife, he sliced the plastic off the other tray, cut the meat into chunks, put it on a saucer.

'Sounds good.' Then her perky voice altered. 'Ooh,' she almost crooned, the sound washing through him like liquid sex, causing his hand to slip on the knife. 'You didn't have to go to so much trouble for Charlie. I've got plenty of cat food.'

He set the saucer on the floor, noticing a pair of bare feet approach as he did so. 'I won't be making a habit of it,' he muttered. She had gold nail polish on her toes, he noticed, with little black snowflakes in the middle of each. Slim ankles, shapely calves—

Four white furry paws bounded into view and the feet moved away as he straightened up to clear the empty meat tray, but Didi got there first.

'Cameron. That steak wasn't for Charlie, was it?' She was smoothing out the plastic wrap and checking the price sticker. 'Come on, fess up. Even with your wealth you wouldn't pay mega bucks for a cat's dinner. You wouldn't pay for a cat's dinner at all if you had your way.'

To his chagrin he watched her lean over the counter top and check out the second container: the gourmet meal. 'Hey, I'm guessing you took out the wrong container. So you made a mistake—no big deal.' She grinned at him through silky gold lashes, her eyes slightly unfocused. 'Why do you feel you need to play Mr Perfecto in your own home? There's only you and me here.'

He was all too aware of that fact, which for some reason had every hair on his body rising, not to mention his blood pressure, and other bodily parts.

He snatched the empty container and plastic out from beneath her hands, catching a whiff of alcohol on her breath as he dumped them in the kitchen bin. Was the woman tipsy on one glass?

'Maintain the Image, perhaps?' she went on when he didn't reply, waving one end of her chiffon scarf. 'I bet you maintain that Mr Perfecto image in your sleep. All buttoned up and stiff...'

Registering the tiny hitch in her breath, he swivelled his head to see her soft cheeks suffused with instant colour. *Right on the mark.*

He turned away, moved to the sink to rinse the mugs left over from breakfast and said the first thing that sprang to his lips. 'What do you feel like eating?'

'Whatever you're having.' Her voice had dropped a notch, turned husky.

His fingers slipped on the mug he was drying as her words slid over him, through him. Ropes of fire snaked along his veins, tugging at his libido, stampeding his imagination into savage, steamy life. Didi riding him, her hair wild, long legs spurring him on, unbuttoning his image with quick deft hands...

He closed his eyes. Very carefully set the mug down. Unclenched his teeth. Wiped his hands on the towel and sent up a silent prayer for sanity.

No doubt about it, she was tipsy. What had he been thinking, giving her champagne on an empty stomach? *That's it, focus on practicalities.* 'You didn't eat lunch,' he barked. 'I told you to help yourself.'

'I forgot.'

Next he knew she'd planted her butt on the bench beside him. He didn't know how she'd got there—one moment she was standing behind him safely out of his line of vision, the next moment she was on the counter top. Perhaps she flew.

He made the mistake of looking at her. Astute silver eyes stared back at him. She wasn't worried about losing her commission or her accommodation, he realised—as he'd already said, he needed her. And they both knew it.

Leaning one elbow alongside her on the counter top, he forced himself to hold her gaze. *Ignore the normal red-blooded male's reaction.* The one still racking his system.

But he *was* a normal red-blooded male. And the warmth of her skin, fair and fresh and fragrant, teased him, tempting him to reach out and touch. He curled his fingers, confining the urge, shooting temptation straight to his already tormented lower body.

Plump rosy lips curved ever so slightly, hinted at a sense of fun. He hadn't experienced anything remotely funny in a long time. When was the last time he'd laughed? Did he even have a sense of humour any more? he wondered. He had the feeling Didi would be the type to breathe life back into it.

Breathe. He could hear the soft sound of her

steady exhalations. Breasts rising, falling... He wanted to look down and see for himself. His fingers itched again to test the weight of her womanly flesh and feel her nipples rise in anticipation against his palms.

A good reason to focus on her face. The eyes brimming with hidden thoughts, the high cheekbones, the neat flat ear lobes— 'You're wearing two different earrings.'

She tipped her head to one side, setting the left one tinkling. 'It's The Look.'

'The look?'

'Asymmetric. Like your Sheila Dodd. Like your tie.' Her eyes dipped and she studied his throat through long silky lashes.

He swallowed over the lump that had suddenly mushroomed from nowhere. 'My tie's asymmetric?'

Wiggling her bottom along the bench until she was within reach, she slotted her fingers behind it, loosening the knot and yanking the silk sideways in one swift movement. 'It is now.' Grinning, she smoothed it all the way down his chest, her eyes following the path of her fingers, every part of his body responding to the touch. 'That's better. It looked like it was strangling you.'

Perceptive girl. Or maybe it was blazingly obvious, he thought, reaching up now to undo the top button of his shirt. He'd never thought this apartment overly warm. Until this woman had turned the heat up.

'Okay. I made a mistake. I intended to impress you with my gourmet dinners specially imported from the Six Spice Deli around the corner.'

Now it was he who manoeuvred along the counter top so Didi was directly in front of him, her knees bumping his waist. So he could rest his hands on her hips. So he could look directly into her eyes and say, 'And I'm probably about to make another one,' as he laid his lips on hers.

CHAPTER FIVE

THE first touch of Didi's mouth against his detonated an explosion that knocked Cameron sideways and shattered the illusion that control was his rock-solid foundation, that he could pull away any time.

Sparks. They sizzled along his nerves with the spectacular ferocity of frayed power cables, snapping and crackling through his blood, sending his hormones spearing into the sky like some crazed Eureka Tower.

He felt her instant response—the heave of her breasts as she struggled to drag in air and push him away, then her mouth softening, opening, hands rising to clutch at his shirt. The moan deep in her throat as he changed the angle for better access.

Her taste was a sweet temptation, luring him deeper to sample the dark lusciousness of her tongue, to drink in its hot honey flavour as it writhed with his.

This was no ordinary kiss. This was the force of a wrecking ball at its most dramatic, splintering thought and crumbling to dust barriers he'd thought impenetrable.

Had he thought himself immune to emotion? He tried telling himself this was a severe case of lust but somehow the condition sounded grossly inadequate. Because something else was happening here. Something he didn't want to think about because if he did he'd know he'd made a bigger mistake than he'd ever dreamed of.

Instead he pulled her closer, shifted nearer, between thighs that seemed to melt apart at his wordless command so he could feel her sultry heat seep through his shirt and into his skin.

Her softness yielded to his burgeoning hardness, hot blood beating through his body as his hands slid from her hips to the curve of her bottom and found the hem of her T-shirt. Fingers barely steady crept beneath to find smooth alabaster skin, the delicate arch of her spine as she leaned into him.

Her grip on his shirt tightened. Jersey-clad legs clamped around his waist, locking their lower bodies in an iron embrace. He rocked against her. Sweat broke out on his brow, his lungs seized.

The urge to rip away the thin barrier and drive into her—right here, right now, without thought for the consequences—

He wrenched his mouth away from her satiny warmth. Backed up a step. It was torture to slide his hands beneath her thighs, over firm shapely calves and untangle her legs from around him. Madness to look into her wide silver eyes and see his own ardour reflected back. Had he forgotten so soon? Lust was one thing, this emotional whatever it was…was something else.

He didn't do emotion. Not since Katrina.

Chewing on passion-plumped lips, she drew in a breath, her breasts rising with the effort, drawing his attention to her nipples outlined clearly against her T-shirt.

'A-a-ah.' Her breathy voice drew the sound out like spun toffee.

'I—' A stab of pain in his lower leg cut through his senses and he stumbled back a step. 'What the…?'

Charlie. He glared down at the cat, who'd apparently polished off his silver-service main course and decided trouser-clad legs were a convenient dessert.

'What?' Didi still had a death-grip on his shirt

and now one of the animal's damn claws seemed to be lodged tight in the leg of his Armani trousers. He teetered dangerously for a couple of seconds before rocking forward on the balls of his feet only to feel one shoe land on something squishy.

'Bloody cat.' He shook his leg free and the animal bounded away with a hiss of annoyance, no doubt in search of its next victim of choice—the French silk drapes, perhaps.

His body still pulsed, his leg throbbed, his pride was dust beneath his feet. There was a rip in the fabric and—he checked—a disgusting disc of squashed fillet steak on the bottom of his shoe.

He looked back at Didi, who'd relinquished her hold on his shirt to cup her hands over her mouth and nose. 'It's okay,' he reassured her. 'Hardly a scratch.'

Didi stared at Cameron while she tried to regain control of her runaway emotions. Her lips felt as if they'd been buzzed by a supersonic jet; her pulse was galloping for a win in the Melbourne Cup.

Alcohol on an empty stomach had snatched away reason and common sense. Planting her butt on the counter top had been her first mistake.

He looked…worried? No, he looked confused.

Blame the champers for the fit of giggles that bub-
bled up her throat. She must be borderline loony
because why would she feel like laughing when
she'd just been kissed senseless and he was probably going to kill her cat and fire her and life was
never going to be the same again?

She couldn't help it; the half-laugh, half-cough
tumbled out, convulsive and slightly hysterical.

His gaze narrowed slightly, his bemused expression didn't alter. 'Are you laughing?'

'I'm sorry, it's just...' She dabbed at her eyes
with the corner of her scarf. Her sudden amusement faded as he bent and she saw him twitch at
the hem of his trouser leg to inspect the damage
to his flesh—twin stripes of red. 'Are you okay?'

He grabbed a tissue, moistened it under the tap
and dabbed at the wound. 'I'm probably going to
die of blood poisoning or tetanus but don't let that
spoil your evening.'

'Let's have a look.' She slid off the bench but he
was scraping meat from the bottom of his shoe
and she couldn't see. 'Where's your first-aid box?'

'I don't need first aid. Or maybe I do, but not for
my leg.' He straightened and met her eyes. 'What
just happened here—'

'Was a kiss, Cameron.'

At least that was what she'd thought it was. But she'd never thought a simple kiss by the kind of man you'd sworn to avoid could suck the air from your lungs and leave you in need of an oxygen mask. Burn you from the inside out until you were cinders. Send your heart spinning in a thousand different directions until you didn't know which way was up. The answer: it wasn't a simple kiss. Which only led to another question: what *was* it?

But she was hardly going to tell him all that, was she? The best option was to feign nonchalance. As if she exchanged saliva with almost-strangers every day of the week. So she shrugged. 'It was fun, Cameron.'

'Fun.' His tone mocked and his eyes, darkly assessing, pinned her own, holding her immobile, stripping away clothes, flesh and façade until she understood the meaning of naked to the core.

It took all her strength to drag her eyes away. 'My guess would be you thought so too,' she managed, whirling away to drag open cupboards. 'About that first-aid box...'

But she could feel his gaze tracking her movements, like a hot glue gun oozing heat down her spine, her bottom, her legging-clad thighs.

Suddenly he was behind her. She felt his shirt

brush her sleeve, his breath against her bare arm as she reached for the next cupboard. Her heart rate, barely back to something approaching normal, picked up pace once more.

Then he leaned closer, the hard planes of his chest abrading her spine, her nape, the back of her head as he reached to the top shelf. She could smell the residue of cologne he'd used this morning, and, beneath that, the scent of soap and man. This man. She'd smell it in her sleep tonight, and a few nights more. Many nights more.

'Here,' he snapped. Rather than the super-dooper kit she expected, he pulled out an old ice-cream tub with a loose assortment of Band-Aids, painkillers, tubes and bottles. He stepped back and Didi swayed at the sudden loss of contact. Her head was spinning, her legs felt numb.

He lifted out a tube of antiseptic cream, barely glanced at her as he said, 'Looks like you should sit down. Or perhaps you should eat.' He flicked his head at the counter top. 'There's a dinner there. It should still be hot.'

Probably a sensible idea, even if her stomach churned at the thought of food. 'I think I will.' She peeled off the lid, grabbed a spoon, filled a tumbler of water and perched on a kitchen bar stool at the end of the counter top. But even the fragrance of sweet-spiced Moroccan lamb didn't tempt her appetite out of hiding.

She dug out a token chickpea or two, rolled them around her mouth, barely swallowed. Gulped water. Then the sight of Cameron placing one foot on a chair, rolling up his trouser leg and exposing one firm calf with thick masculine hair dried her mouth all over again.

The two distinct raised welts were dealt with swiftly and she stared as he rubbed in antiseptic cream with long blunt fingers.

Dark olive skin overlaid the hard muscle. Her own fingers tingled and her creativity took flight. Oh, how would it feel to run her hands up his leg? What was it about this guy? She'd never even looked at Jay this way. This wicked, wanton way.

She'd take off his shoe, his sock. Start at the toes and work her way up. From the smooth skin of his instep to the rougher skin above the sock line. She'd watch his eyes darken to that gorgeous blueberry as she crept her fingers higher, beneath the trousers to fondle his kneecap. Higher, where the tops of his thighs would be hard, like wood, then to the inner thigh where it would be softer, hotter…

'How is it?'

His voice penetrated the sexual shroud she found herself immersed in. As she blinked it away she became aware of her own heart beating a thick, heavy rhythm against her ribs. Aware of his eyes studying her with a searing intensity that made her wonder if he could read her thoughts.

She managed a smile, hoped it looked casual and tried for light. 'Mmm, good. Want a taste?'

His gaze dropped to her mouth, the sexual glitter in his eyes making her lips feel swollen and sensual, as if she'd invited him to taste something far more intimate. A taste he'd already acquainted himself with, and her pulse spiked at the memory.

Which was probably why he said, 'Thanks, but I'll eat later. When I've finished at the office.' He rolled down his trouser leg, capped the tube. He didn't want an encore. In fact she got the distinct feeling he did, in fact, consider it a mistake, as he'd said before he kissed her.

She told herself she was *not* disappointed. She did *not* need another reminder of her own mistakes. Rather, she felt a growing unease that he was leaving his own apartment on her account. Guilt because he shouldn't have to do that. She set the spoon on the counter top with a chink of silver on granite. 'I thought you'd finished for the day?'

'I've got some last-minute details to finalise before I leave for Sydney.'

'You're going to Sydney?'

'First thing in the morning. I'm viewing some glass figurines and wooden carvings I intend purchasing for the gallery. I'll be gone a couple of days. You'll be okay here alone, won't you?'

He didn't pause for an answer, just dragged a wallet from the back pocket of his trousers, pulled out a couple of business cards and a wad of fifty-dollar bills. 'I haven't had time to organise a credit card but this should cover your expenses while I'm away. I use a limo service; I'll let them know the car's at your disposal.' He counted the cash, laid it on the table.

She stared. She'd never seen anyone lay down such a large amount of cash at one time and not blink an eye. Perhaps it simply wasn't enough for him to bother about. 'You're not afraid I'll do a runner with your money?'

He shook his head once. 'You'll hang out for the prize. You stand to earn ten times that amount— and earn a name for yourself at the same time.' Spoken with an almost indiscernible disdain for those beneath his privileged position of wealth and power. She recognised it and anger flared, hot and harsh. 'How dare you presume to pigeonhole me—or anyone else for that matter—because I don't live at a fancy address?'

He flashed her a look, a cold blue flame that froze and burned, holding her in its grip for a few tense heartbeats, and for a gut-curdling moment a stranger seemed to stare back at her. *He's not the man you think he is.* The poster pinned to the ladies' room mirror streaked through her mind.

She slid off the stool and took a step back, rubbing arms that suddenly felt chilled. Who was this man she'd committed herself to work for? Whose apartment she'd be living in for the next couple of weeks?

The man who'd kissed her with toe-curling expertise.

The man she'd kissed back.

His gaze relented a little but his face remained stony and unforgiving, the lines around his mouth suddenly looked deeper. 'You're mistaken,' he said quietly. 'I judge people by the way they live their life, not their address.'

'I'm—'

'Any problems, speak to Davis downstairs or

call my mobile.' He turned and headed to the dining room, collected his jacket.

Trailing in his wake, Didi nodded, hugging her own threatened security within her crossed arms.

As he shrugged into his jacket he said, 'If you're cold, turn up the thermostat; it's on the wall by the front door.'

'I'm not cold.' Just uncertain.

'I'll be late back tonight and gone early. Have some work in progress for me to look at when I get back.'

'I will.' Spoken with a certain amount of trepidation.

He paused, looking grimly awkward. 'We should clear the air about that moment...'

She was almost tempted to let him bumble through an explanation, but, really, she didn't want to discuss it either. 'I told you, it was a bit of fun. Let's leave it at that.'

He nodded and she sensed his relief. His remote expression relaxed into some semblance of the guy who'd toasted their partnership with her less than an hour ago. 'See you on Friday.'

Then he was gone. Didi sank into the nearest available sofa. She hoped her creativity wasn't shot to pieces. Charlie wandered in, jumped up onto her lap and began purring, bumping his head against her hand. 'There you are. You just wanted in on the action, didn't you? Or were you jealous, hey? Well, you don't have to worry, there won't be any more.' Cameron's kiss might be the hottest thing since supernovae were discovered but they'd never be compatible.

Except in bed.

She had no doubt he'd be an absolute god in bed. But he'd never be suitable in the ways that counted. Yet she hardly knew him, how could she make any kind of judgement?

Well, she knew some things. He'd never understand what it was like to wonder where your next dollar was coming from or where you were going to sleep tonight. Mind you, neither had she until she'd made the decision to go it alone.

'Don't bother coming back until you're prepared to take your place as a part of our family and communicate rationally,' her mother had said when Didi had flounced into the lounge room and announced she was leaving. Fitting in with her family's lifestyle had never suited her. A lifestyle Cameron Black would be totally at home with.

But who was he really? With his lifestyle, looks, his way with women, he reminded her too much of the man who, to her humiliation, had left her to cancel their wedding plans alone. But she'd seen glimpses—shadows—of someone else behind that polished façade. Drained of energy, she closed her eyes. Cameron Black Property Developers might have a reputable name but Cameron Black, the man, was someone else entirely.

The wide steel doors slid open on a cushion of air and Cam stepped into his night-darkened office on the fifteenth floor with its twinkling vista of lights below, but he barely gave them a glance as he strode past the empty reception area. He'd kissed her. Didi. The woman he'd commissioned to work for him.

Why, for God's sake? Because he'd been unable to help himself. He'd been bewitched. No, he told himself, it was simpler than that—he was horny. Scowling, he rifled through his files until he found the Sydney contacts. She didn't call the shots where his sex life was concerned. So why had it felt as if he'd been sledgehammered? As if he'd been the one out of control?

He tossed the necessary paperwork into his briefcase then moved to his computer, booted it up. He'd not go to Sydney next weekend as he'd originally planned, but tomorrow.

Just a kiss. That was all it was, right?

Who knew what might have happened if the damn cat hadn't decided to take a piece out of him?

Sex might have happened.

Fast furious sex on his kitchen counter. The image of him whipping her leggings down and plunging himself into that warm wet heat had his pulse stepping up, his blood rushing to his groin. He swore. He didn't do emotional, he didn't do trust, not where women were concerned. Not any more.

He tapped keys, booked a seat on the six a.m. flight and printed out his boarding pass. He wanted the best Didi could do with her *needlework.* He needed her creativity on the wall, not in his bed.

Didi spent the following morning designing something on paper, deciding on materials, sorting through what she already had and what she needed to purchase.

This was what she needed to concentrate her thoughts on, she told herself as she pulled out skeins of tangerine and vermilion silk and matched them to the aubergine. Not the sexy man who was paying her, offering her the chance she'd been waiting for.

Next she took Cameron's offer of the limo service and shopped like a queen—for supplies. But it was liberating selecting materials without having to think of the cost. Paying for them with the cash he'd left, then riding back to his apartment without having to depend on an unreliable car, the hassles of parking or public transport. The carefree way she'd done as a child.

She and her sister had been raised as the privileged daughters of a society couple. Their parents graced the social pages regularly and she'd attended numerous functions over the years. As a teenager, she'd accompanied her mother to her charitable events, had witnessed firsthand what it was like to live in the gutter with no support, no hope. She'd seen the despair in those eyes and what that desperation led to—drugs, crime, death. It had changed the way Didi viewed her place in the world.

Over the years she'd devoted regular early mornings to helping out with the kids' breakfast club on the seamier side of the city, lent her expertise to an arts programme for women and children in shelters, volunteered late shifts at a halfway house for those undergoing drug rehabilitation.

People were all equals as far as Didi was concerned.

Mum didn't see it that way. *They're not like us, dear.* Her mother would tell Didi, 'It's our duty as Christians to help those less fortunate than ourselves.' But she didn't want to soil her silk ensembles doing it.

Nor could Didi imagine Cameron Black getting his designer suits dirty in a soup kitchen or handing out blankets to the homeless on a frosty night.

Bulging shopping bags hanging from both arms, she stepped onto the footpath in front of his apartment building, glancing at a young woman at the entrance as she passed. Even in skinny jeans and a casual black velvet jacket, she was stunning. At around six foot, she was a statuesque brunette with clear blue eyes. Yes, she'd fit right in amongst the tenants who resided here, Didi thought.

Whereas she'd never fitted in. Her older sister, Veronica, took after their parents—tall, dark. Immaculate. At eighteen she'd married a wealthy middle-aged owner of several luxury yachts that ferried rich tourists around the Harbour and now lived a life of luxury in one of Sydney's most affluent suburbs.

She nodded to Davis at the security desk and crossed the ornate foyer, stepped into the elevator. If her sister could see Didi now…

Should she answer that? Didi frowned at her mobile over her glasses while the familiar tune rang out over the soft CD she'd been working to. She didn't need any distractions, but what if it was Cameron checking up on her with some request or other? She could tell him she'd started, even if she didn't need to hear his deep velvet voice on the other end of the line. She set down the frame she was in the process of constructing and answered with a crisp, 'Hello?'

'Surprise!'

'Veronica?' Thinking of the devil in Prada had somehow conjured her up. Didi leaned back in her chair, removed her glasses, stunned to hear her sister's voice. Veronica hadn't spoken to her since she'd left Sydney. She rarely spoke to Didi in any case, unless it was to denigrate her. So why was she ringing now? Didi rubbed the frown pleating her brow. 'How are you?'

'I'm well. Are you busy?' When Didi didn't

answer, Veronica said, 'I didn't know if you'd be able to take personal calls while you're working. Some work-places have a strict policy on mobile phones. I was going to leave a message.'

'Ah-h-h... No, it's cool.' The little lie tripped off her tongue—as far as her family knew, she worked in a gallery and she wanted to keep it that way. 'We're fairly casual here.'

'Great. Listen, I'm in Melbourne for a couple of days—Daniel's at a residential conference in Brisbane and I told him I needed a break to explore Melbourne's shopping arcades. And to see you of course,' she added. It sounded like an afterthought. Definitely an afterthought.

More like you're checking up on me. Didi's stomach dived to her feet as her hand tightened on the phone. 'You're in Melbourne? *Now?*' Oh, she was so dead.

'I'm at the airport. I should be in the city in, say, thirty minutes. What's the gallery's address? I'll come straight there.'

'No!' *Think.*

'What's wrong?' A definite edge of suspicion. 'I'll only stay a few moments. We can catch up after—'

'I'm not actually working at the gallery today...'

She paused, looked around at *her apartment*. Cameron wasn't due home till tomorrow night. He'd never know Veronica had set foot in the place. 'I'm working from home,' she continued. 'I've been commissioned to do a piece for the opening of a new gallery.' That part was true, at least.

'Oh…that's…great.'

She heard her sister's tentative approval and breathed a sigh of almost-relief. Her sister could go home and report everything was fine with Didi and maybe, just maybe, her family would accept her choice and let her back into their lives again without disgrace. She gave her Cameron's address. 'Speak to Security, they'll buzz you through.'

'I can't wait to see this new apartment and it'll give us time to catch up. I'll stay overnight if that's okay.'

'Oh…' A jolt of alarm shot through her, and she sprang out of her chair. 'Fine,' she finished faintly. What else could she say? 'See you soon.'

Two bedrooms. Veronica could sleep in the room she'd been using.

Which left Didi with Cameron's room…

CHAPTER SIX

SHE stabbed the disconnect button and flew towards the hall. Did she dare…? *No choice.*

Swiftly she gathered up her meagre supply of clothes and toiletries and lugged them down to Cameron's room. But she paused at the closed door. She'd never been in here. She'd barely seen past the crack in the door on her way past.

She had thirty minutes tops.

As she flung the door open the cedar-wood scent of his cologne wafted past her. She stood a moment breathing it in while she cast her eyes over the room. A stunning view of nearby high-rise buildings cast a reflected afternoon glow on the cream carpet and deep blue quilt atop the king-sized bed. Matching drapes graced floor-to-ceiling windows, which opened onto a balcony filled with soft ferns.

A partially open door revealed an en-suite bathroom in cream and gold. Shuffling to the far side with her arms full, she pulled open a cupboard door and discovered it led to a walk-in wardrobe filled with racks of top designer suits and enough pressed shirts to last a year.

In what seemed another life she'd had a cupboard like this. She'd given her designer labels to charity, walked away from her family's disapproval to become an artist. It was vital Veronica thought Didi successful.

She stuffed her clothes next to a rack of shiny leather shoes, then moved to the bathroom, swept Cameron's toiletries out of sight beneath the vanity and arranged her own. Just in case...

And tomorrow morning her sister would be gone—Didi would see to it personally, even if it meant accompanying Veronica on her shopping spree and waving her off to the airport in a taxi.

At the cost of having something for Cameron to look at?

She shook the disturbing thought away. She'd roughed out a plan, hadn't she? She'd bought supplies, put together a frame to work on. The sound of the elevator doors alerted her and she hurried from Cameron's room, closing the door.

'Hi.' Didi gave Veronica a quick hug and took charge of her suitcase.

'Hmm.' Veronica's eyes swept the apartment. 'I

never imagined this. It must cost you a fortune.' She cast Didi an assessing glance. 'How do you afford it?'

Aware of her tatty jeans and dishevelled hair, Didi noted the classic lines of her sister's designer outfit, the pink suede boots, the perfect make-up and long dark hair salon-streaked with auburn highlights. Was it any wonder Veronica would ask that question? And why hadn't she anticipated an answer?

'Ah, the gallery owner was leasing it out at low cost since he's interstate at present.' Didi, who never lied, who hated deception, was getting in deeper with every passing moment. Spinning on her heel, she set the rolling case in motion. 'Your room's this way. I hope you don't mind sharing it with a cat,' she said over her shoulder.

'Not at all. You know I love cats, but Daniel's allergic, you know.'

She knew. Daniel Davenport was allergic to most things, including anyone remotely connected with poverty. Didi showed Veronica to her room, indicated the bathroom at her disposal, then left her to freshen up.

A few moments later, Veronica appeared, re-questing a tour of the apartment. Didi whisked her through the rooms, then suggested they go out for lunch before hitting the shops.

Veronica spent a fortune; Didi helped her. Later they swapped childhood stories over a leisurely dinner. Even though she wasn't a nightclub fan, Didi suggested they cruise to a couple of nightspots so that by the time they returned home it was well after one a.m.

Didi sighed a breath of relief when Veronica said she was exhausted and intended showering then going to bed. Didi happily agreed to do the same.

As she tiptoed into Cameron's room her skin prickled with the feeling that he was somehow there with her, breathing down her neck. She closed the door behind her and, leaving the light off, wandered to the sliding door that looked out onto the balcony. Ferns shifted in the breeze. Turning, she took in the immaculate room. Shadows and light played over the walls. The sibilance of the air-conditioning overlaid the muted traffic noise.

Even though none of his personal items were visible, his presence lingered. The room smelled of him. How could she possibly get any sleep in here? she wondered, gazing back at the twinkling streetscape below.

A hot shower might help. She stripped off her clothes, tossed them on the bottom of the bed and padded across the carpet in the semi-darkness.

Light flooded the bathroom as she flicked on the switch. She startled at her own reflection, then chastised herself for being foolish. 'Your secret's safe,' she whispered. Why was she whispering, for goodness' sake? 'He's hundreds of kilometres away,' she said out loud to convince herself. 'Only a few more hours and he'll never know.'

She turned on the spray, smothered her face in cleanser, massaging it in until the room began to steam, then stepped under the water's glorious heat.

She'd left her personal soap in the other bathroom. Which meant she had to use Cameron's soap. The one she'd smelled on him last night. As she lathered up and rubbed the slippery suds over her arms and breasts her nipples turned to tight little peaks, blood rising to the surface and turning her skin a blushing pink, reminding her of how he'd made her feel last night.

Hot. Turned on. Every body part excruciatingly sensitive.

She reached for her exfoliating mitt, scrubbed her skin with unnecessary vigour, hoping the harsh abrasive action would relieve the discomfort. No. It merely deepened the blush in places, which gave the appearance of sunburned patchwork.

She yanked off the mitt. This was bad. Worse, this inappropriate preoccupation with Cameron Black had to stop. Right now. Closing her eyes, she leaned back against the cool tiles, lifted her head to the spray and let the water pound her. One more minute…

Cameron frequently employed the element of surprise. He keyed in his entry code and watched the floor numbers illuminate as he rode the elevator towards his apartment. Expect the unexpected—it kept employees on their toes.

The same went for sexy little waitresses who moonlighted as live-in commissioned artists. Still, a buoyant feeling of anticipation lifted him, stirring memories of the last time he'd seen her—deliciously mussed, her lips red-cherry plump. The fact that it had been him plucking the fruit only added to the intensity.

That aside, he knew little about her. He *did* know she kept him second-guessing, stimulated him with her bubbly personality and quick tongue.

And, to his never-ending surprise and discomfort, aroused his libido far too frequently.

She had the looks of a pixie but she kissed like an angel.

The reason he'd taken off for Sydney earlier than planned. The fact that she'd called that moment in the kitchen 'fun' merely demonstrated the type of woman she was—carelessly casual. That *was* the type of woman he preferred now, wasn't it? So the fact that it had rocked him more than it had her was disturbing in the extreme and best forgotten.

He needed to keep his distance, put some perspective on the situation, he assured his muted reflection in the impersonal elevator's mirrored walls. No way was he going to jeopardise this commission; it was too important. He was taking a risk on an unknown, probably paying her far more than he should. He didn't even know if she was up for the task at such short notice.

He'd been naïve to trust a woman he barely knew in his apartment with a load of cash. Which was why he'd decided to return a day earlier.

Not for any burning desire to see her again.

The elevator doors swished open, heightening that sense of anticipation. He forced himself to concentrate on important matters. If she was asleep, he could view her work at leisure without her looking over his shoulder and distracting him.

Light from the hallway beckoned. She wasn't in bed yet, then. His blood pumped that little bit faster. He turned into the hall—and saw a tall, dark-haired woman in a slim-fitting blue night-gown strolling out of the guest bathroom as if she had every right to be there.

He stilled, every hair on his body rising as a fierce disappointment stabbed through him. He'd been right to come home early. The moment his back was turned Didi was entertaining guests. He supposed he should be relieved it wasn't a male. But she'd abused his trust, something he couldn't, *wouldn't* tolerate.

The woman came to an abrupt halt, clutching a bag of toiletries to her breasts, dark eyes wary. 'Who are you and what are you doing here?'

'I live here,' he said grimly. 'Who the hell are you?'

'Dymphna's sister.'

'Dim…*who?*'

'Didi,' she clarified. Her disparaging gaze swept over him despite the fact he wore well-pressed trousers and a sky-blue business shirt. 'She didn't say anything about a boarder.'

'Boarder.' The word exploded from his mouth. 'She said that?'

She shook her head. 'I already told you, she didn't mention anyone else living here, so, no, she didn't say that.'

'No, I don't suppose she did.' A red haze shimmered before his eyes. She wouldn't. Not if she wanted to play lady of the manor, or whatever her game was, in his apartment.

The woman moved swiftly towards Didi's room, keeping close to the wall. 'I'm calling Security if you don't identify yourself.'

'Go ahead. In fact, I'll call them for you.' Keeping his eye on her, he backed up to the security panel in the wall, hit the button. 'Davis, Cam Black here. There's a woman in my apartment calling herself—what's your name?'

'Veronica Davenport.'

Cam listened while Davis explained that Miss O'Flanagan had a guest staying overnight and enquired was everything all right.

'Fine,' Cam clipped, and disconnected.

'Not Veronica O'Flanagan, then.' He studied her from the top of her shiny dark hair to the tips of her manicured toenails, saw her register the fact that he knew Didi's surname.

The woman reeked of wealth. The kind of inherited wealth Cam despised. It didn't fit. Didi was nothing like this model of sophistication in any way, shape or form.

'Davenport's my married name.' She tilted her head so that she looked down her nose at him, but he didn't miss the appreciative way she cast her eyes over his body. 'You haven't explained yet who *you* are.'

No, I haven't, have I? 'Where's Didi now?' he demanded. He strolled to the entrance to Didi's room, blocking the other woman's path and casting a quick glance inside. The bed was empty and he could see an open Louis Vuitton suitcase on the floor by the window.

'She's gone to bed.' She indicated behind him with a stiff tilt of her head.

His room.

His whole body stiffened. Didi was sleeping in his room? In his bed, between his sheets. Heat and anger warred within him but desire snaked through the mix like a restless serpent in a stormy sea. He moved away from the door, gestured her inside. 'Then I suggest you do the same, since you're obviously spending the night.'

'Not until you identify yourself to my satisfaction. How do I know you're not here to do my sister harm?'

He pulled out his driver's licence, flashed it at her. 'I told you—I live here. You want to speak to Security yourself, be my guest. Otherwise do as I ask. Leave Didi to me. I assure you, she's perfectly safe.' If he didn't throttle her first.

But the woman must have read something in his expression because a small smile twitched at the edge of her mouth, as if she'd just discovered a delicious secret. 'Didi didn't tell me she had a man in her life.'

His jaw clenched at that but he aimed an imperious finger at the door and spoke through stiff lips. 'Goodnight, Veronica.'

Still clutching her toiletry bag and her innate poise—and the smile—she slipped inside with a murmured, 'Goodnight,' and closed the door.

Cameron let out the breath he hadn't realised had backed up in his lungs. Steeling himself for the sight of Didi's tartan pyjama-clad body in his bed, he strode to his room, his traitorous palms tingling in anticipation of waking her.

He didn't knock, shoving at the door with an open-handed *thwack*. The scent of his soap and Melbourne's glimmering skyline through the windows greeted him. He was halfway across the room, arm outstretched to wake her, before he realised that she wasn't in bed. That the sound he could hear wasn't his blood pounding through his ears, it was running water, and that the fragrance billowed from steam clouds through the door of the en-suite.

The partially open door.

Too late to deny what he'd seen. Somehow he dragged his gaze away from the outline of her body in his shower stall, but it was indelibly printed behind his retinas. Her creamy flesh in a pose that rivalled anything in a men's magazine. The swell of her buttocks, the way she'd tipped back her head against the tiles so that her throat arched wantonly. As if waiting for a lover to take a bite. His mouth turned dry, his body hardened.

The water stopped and he heard her open the shower door. He stood rooted to the floor as possible scenarios flashed through his mind in that split second. Stranger. Stalker. She'd scream. Veronica and the cops would join the party.

He took the best option he could think of, given

the circumstances. Diving into the bathroom, he grabbed a towel from the rail and held it in front of her with one hand. He did *not* see the tight rosy nipples, the cute little belly button, the erotic patch at the juncture of her thighs.

Her eyes widened and predictably she opened her mouth but his free hand got there first, clamping on damp, petal-soft skin. 'Didi. It's Cameron. Don't scream.'

Her shoulders relaxed a little but he watched as her predicament dawned on her and they tensed right back up again. She struggled to cover herself with the towel, her breath hot on his palm as she made a noise of distress.

He felt her delicate jawbone tense beneath his fingers but his hold didn't slacken. 'Don't,' he warned. 'Veronica'll have my balls for breakfast.'

Her lashes flickered at that and she nodded, continuing to watch him steadily. Satisfied she wasn't going to cause a ruckus, he relaxed his hand a little but he didn't want to let her go quite yet. He was enjoying her rare quietness and it gave him a moment to think how he was going to handle this.

Drops of water lay on her flushed skin, her hair, her eyelashes. The knowledge that she'd used his personal soap on her body spun through his head like an aphrodisiac. She was clutching the towel to her breasts, pushing them higher. He watched as a single droplet fell from her hair and trickled into that forbidden valley.

It occurred to him that she could have pulled away without too much effort. No doubt she was using the time for reflection and planning her excuses as well. He clenched his jaw and reminded himself that she'd helped herself to his apartment behind his back.

Mind spinning, Didi stared up at the man gripping her jaw and mouth, watching her with a speculative glint in his midnight eyes...and something more...something predatory? And no wonder; dear heaven, he'd seen her naked. How long had he been standing there while she lingered provocatively against the tiles like some hooker?

She shivered as her mind veered in another direction while he continued devouring her with that rapacious expression. He was *here*. In *his* bathroom. *Not* in Sydney.

Oh. My. God. What had she done? And how was she going to *un*do it?

His hand moved away from her mouth but one finger continued to slide sensuously over her lower lip, a dangerous touch, a hypnotic caress that slowed time and wiped everything from her mind but the pleasure it provoked. Beneath their calloused texture she could feel the tension ready to clamp her mouth shut again if she didn't co-operate.

His voice held the same deceptively languid quality when he said, 'So, Didi…or should I call you Dymphna?'

Her whole body rebelled and she speared him with her eyes. 'Don't call me that—never call me that.'

His mouth curved slightly. 'I agree it's a crime to punish an innocent child with such a name. Then again…' he whisked his thumb back and forth over her jaw, firmed his other hand against the back of her head, imprisoning her '…maybe it isn't such a crime… Maybe you're not so innocent.'

In the room's dimness the lights from a nearby skyscraper stroked the unyielding angle of his jaw, his eyes mesmerised her, his grasp on her head paralysed her. His finger continued to fondle the edge of her lip, sending shivery tingles to every extremity and sparking erotic images of letting him use that same lazy thoroughness to explore other body parts. She fought an insane urge to suck its pleasure-giving warmth into her mouth.

'Well, are you going to try and defend yourself?' His tone sharper, eyes piercing. 'Or maybe I'll tell you what I think and you can try to deny it.'

She shook her head but it didn't move beneath his grip. 'I didn't expect you back until tomorrow night.' Her voice came out hoarse and pitifully desperate.

'That was the original plan.'

'I'm sorry. My sister flew into Melbourne unexpectedly. I told her I live here, that I work in a gallery, which is all a lie, I know. You weren't here, I didn't think it would matter—just for one night, Cameron.' The familiar sting of rejection, the secret heartache of not belonging, washed through her. 'But it matters to me.' Unshed tears pricked at her eyes. 'That she thinks I'm a success, that my family thinks I'm a success.'

There was a softening in his eyes, as if he…understood her. His hold loosened a little, though his hand continued to massage the back of her head, and a rare, wry humour lifted the corner of his mouth. 'She *thinks* I'm your lover.'

The image ran through her like quicksilver. Too

easy with her head cradled in his expert hand to let herself remember what had happened in the kitchen… 'She…does?' Well, naturally she would since there was only one other bedroom…

She sensed his mood lighten and her own initial fears thawed a little. He'd invested a heap of money in her already. He wouldn't turf her out until the job was finished. Would he? No, she assured herself, he didn't have time to find a replacement. Question was, could she negotiate with only a towel held to her breasts?

She stepped back. He let her, and she used the opportunity to wrap and secure the towel around her. 'Can we play along with this here? It's only one night—she'll be gone tomorrow.'

'Play.' The way he said it made kindergarten sound like an orgy. Then a dark brow lifted. 'You mean lie.'

She bit her lip. 'Just a little bit. Just for tonight. You don't know how important this is.'

'Why don't you tell me?'

'Later.' After they'd sorted out the logistics of how they were both going to share the room for the night. 'Right now I need you. And you need me.'

'Didi?' Veronica's voice in the hallway. In the

doorway. Even in the semi-darkness, the light from the bathroom illuminated concern—or was it suspicion?—on the familiar face.

Didi's hands tightened on the edge of the towel. Her gaze flicked up to Cameron's, silently pleading with him, to her sister. Back to Cameron.

'Are you all right, Didi? Is this man—?'

'She's fine.' Cameron's hands closed over Didi's upper arms, rubbing seductive circles over her shoulders with hard flat palms, a conspiratorial gleam in his eyes. 'Aren't you, Fairybread?'

Fairy bread? 'Fine,' she managed, holding his gaze, ignoring her sister. She stretched her stiff lips into a smile. 'Now that you're home.' She didn't even have to try to make her voice husky— that gleam in Cameron's eyes, the feel of his hands on her flesh did that.

'That's my girl.' He smiled back, his thumbs massaging the sensitive place where shoulder met torso as he pulled her flush against his hard, lean body. 'Goodnight again, Veronica.'

And leaning down he pressed a firm, open-mouthed kiss on Didi's surprised mouth. His tongue slid across the seam, coaxing her to open, dipping inside when her jaw dropped. Just a tantalising taste, an appetiser, and oh…it felt…good.

But she couldn't allow herself to enjoy it—this was an act, a show. A skilfully executed piece of theatre for her sister's benefit.

She could feel Veronica's stunned gaze. Didi was no less than one hundred and ten per cent stunned herself. Her nipples rasped against the towel, making them throb as he shifted his body for a better fit. *Don't be fooled—this isn't real.*

'If you're sure…' Veronica's voice seemed to float at the edge of Didi's consciousness.

'She's very sure,' Cameron muttered against her mouth.

A moment later Didi heard the swish of her sister's gown and her bedroom door clicked shut. Releasing her arms as suddenly as he'd taken her, he stepped back, withdrawing the warmth of his body with him. But while he'd put physical distance between them, the intensity of his gaze completely possessed her.

A shaft of heat knifed through her. Could he be…turned on by a ten-second performance?

His eyes didn't leave hers as he strode to the door, kicked it shut. Her damp skin prickled in the draught he'd created. As he approached her he shrugged out of his suit jacket, let it fall where

it would. Yanked off his tie, tossed it behind him.
Undid the buttons of his cuffs.

What did he intend? *Isn't it obvious?* a tiny voice
whispered. A shiver of doubt snuck through the
heat. Her fingers crept over the top of her towel,
needing to keep herself secure, protected. 'Um…
thanks…' She flicked a finger, couldn't manage
the hand. 'For…that.'

He didn't reply. He just kept coming, like an approaching storm, big and dark and all-powerful,
making her feel insignificant, a fugitive with no
place to hide.

His hands curled over hers on the towel, knuckles rough against the swell of her still-throbbing
breasts and his eyes turned molten, lightning on
cobalt.

'What was that about needing me, Didi?'

CHAPTER SEVEN

DIDI'S breath snagged mid-chest. She gulped in air. 'I said…we…both needed *one another*…' Oh, cripes…with Cameron's hands covering hers covering her breasts and his gaze hotter than hell's kitchen that did *not* come out sounding the way she'd intended. 'I mean I think we need to discuss…I nee—have to explain…'

Her words—indeed her entire brain function—seized up as he lowered his head again. 'Tell you what, why don't you shut up for a bit?'

His breath feathered across her brow, her cheeks. She could smell fresh winter rain on his clothes, the foresty scent of his aftershave. As if her head were being manipulated by some invisible puppeteer, it tilted up, her lips opening of their own volition. Waiting, trembling…

She had a glimpse of eyes, dark and bright with purpose, a frown of concentration—or was it something else?—between heavily lowered brows before his mouth met hers once more and her eyes slid shut.

This time his tongue didn't linger around the edges of her mouth, it delved inside, seeking, exploring, finding hers. His flavour filled her mouth. She already knew how he tasted but this was more. Now she experienced, not only the flavours of peppermint and coffee, but the exhilarating essence of desire that slid like sun-warmed silk over her tongue, her teeth, inside her lower lip.

His hands left hers to better hold her head, to whisk his fingers over cheeks and jaw, leaving her own hands free to touch his shirt, absorb its crisp feel against her fingertips. To feel the steel muscles of his stomach tighten as she flattened then curled her hands against him.

To feel the quickened tempo of his breathing, his chest expanding as his hands left her head to slide over her shoulders, the shh as they shimmied over the towel, warmth from his palms stroking her, lower, lower. Her limbs turned to jelly, her brain liquefied and she felt herself dissolving against him. Total meltdown…

He lifted his head the tiniest bit. 'Do you need me, Didi?' he murmured, seduction oozing from the words.

She heard herself murmur something unintelligible back. Was that her voice all deep and drowsy and detached, as if it came from somewhere outside her?

'Do you need me to touch you…' she jolted, her hands whipping back to hug the security of her towel when she felt his fingers curl under the hem to touch the bare flesh of her thigh '…here?'

Her eyes snapped open to find his eyes focused on hers. She didn't answer. Couldn't. Holding her breath as his hand glided towards her inner thigh, calluses at the base of his fingers creating a delicious friction and sending shivers spiralling from his touch. Moisture swamped her most feminine place.

His hand changed direction, sliding slowly, inexorably towards the source of that moisture, every second an exercise in torture, every inch a scandalous pleasure. She sucked in a breath but there wasn't any oxygen, only hot airless space filled with his scent. Then her breathing stalled completely as his thumb found the source of her heat, the pinnacle of her pleasure.

'Or maybe you need me here…' He prodded the swollen knot of need with gentle pressure.

'Ah-h-h…' Oh, yes, right…*there.* She shuddered

on the edge of the world, unable to look away from his eyes glittering in the muted light from the bathroom. His facial muscles bunched, his lips firmed, then curved ever so slightly in the knowledge that he'd taken her to the brink of no return with a single flick of his wrist.

It was humiliating to realise that at this moment the man had total and absolute control over her mind and body. But somewhere in her semi-coherent brain a fragment of sanity still clung. 'No,' she whispered, knowing her eyes made a liar of her. Knowing the engorged knot throbbing wantonly against him made a mockery of her.

He wiggled his thumb. 'Your body's sending me an entirely different message.'

'My body doesn't want to listen to reason,' she said over a parched throat. 'I don't even like you.'

A brief hesitation, then his lips stretched into a smile, and she realised he didn't care one way or the other. 'Since when did that stop two people from enjoying such a mutually satisfying experience?' he said reasonably, continuing to stroke her moisture as she rocked helplessly against him.

She swallowed. *Yeah, since when?* Over his shoulder she saw a gibbous moon sail silently from behind a high-rise, bathing the room in silver light.

'Didi.' He removed his clever hand to tilt her face to his, thumbs rasping over her cheeks, eyes dark with intensity. 'I played along with you, didn't I? Don't you want to convince Veronica I'm the real deal?'

'I think we managed that a few moments ago.'

'Ah, but tomorrow morning she'll be expecting to see the afterglow in your smile.'

'Afterglow…?' Her breath caught as every internal organ leaped up and changed places.

'I promise,' he said. Low and smooth and sexy. Confident. Arrogant, even.

And she had no doubt he could deliver. She shuddered even as she willed those talented fingers to find their way beneath her towel again.

The hot tub of desire in his eyes swirled and swallowed her up. 'Why don't we find out what this thing between us is all about?'

'This *thing?*' This angsty, itchy thing that hadn't given her a decent night's sleep since she'd met him? 'The thing about "things" is they get complicated and someone ends up getting hurt.'

'It doesn't have to be complicated.' He paused. 'Unless there's someone else?'

She glared at him, her back stiffening, shoulders tensing as Jay's image flitted through her mind. 'Would I be standing here naked with you if there was?' *Sweet heaven, naked with Cameron Black.*

He must have read her wistful expression because he looked into her eyes and said, 'Who was he, Didi?'

'Just a guy I…thought I loved.'

'He hurt you. He's scum.'

She bit her lip. 'I'm over him. And I don't want to talk about him.'

She tried to pull away but he held her fast. 'Neither do I.' He tightened his fingers on her cheeks. 'As I said, we can keep this simple. This time we know up front how it's going to be—no one gets hurt.'

She shook her head. 'We have a working relationship—'

His finger on her lips stopped her. 'Work's for tomorrow. So stop analysing, stop talking and for Pete's sakes relax…'

The knot in the towel came undone at his touch. Cool air breathed over her body, a stunning contrast to the heat emanating from his gaze as the towel slid to the floor. He took in every curve, from the hollow at the base of her neck where her pulse beat like horses' hooves, the fullness of her breasts swelling beneath his scrutiny, her waist, the flare of her hips.

'You're a work of art yourself, Ms O'Flanagan.' His voice was smooth and sensual and Didi could imagine he used that self-assured tone with women all the time. But there was something in his eyes reflected in the moon's silver light that hinted at that innate vulnerability she'd seen that night in the ladies' loo before he blinked it away.

He reached out. One fingertip brushed against her neck, over her left breast to draw a circle around the stiff nipple. Another.

Oh-h-h. Her already aroused body hummed with unbearable tension. Seeing him clothed while she stood as naked as a Greek statue was unspeakably erotic. A few more seconds of this protracted torment and she was likely to snap.

'Relax?' She managed, barely, to get the word out. 'Right now this *work of art* is fraying at the edges.'

His hitherto solemn expression transformed to a grin. 'That so?'

'Damn right.' *Don't think about whether this is a wise decision.* Because even if she did, she didn't think she could pull back. Long-suppressed need asserted itself. She took a step closer so that their bodies were a shiver away and poked his chest. 'In fact it's in danger of disintegrating…' Her fingertip discovered a shirt button, found the edge of his shirt, wiggled through to find hard, hairy skin. 'It needs serious attention. Now.'

She emphasised her demand by closing the gap and bumping her body against his. To explore the sensation of cotton against her breasts, the ridge of belt buckle, the coarser weave of fine skin-warmed wool along her thighs.

To spread her prickling palm against the front of his trousers and soothe the itch along every inch of his hard, hot length.

It didn't soothe—neither her nor him. The itch was a virus spreading through her body, as powerful as it was contagious. His sexy grin vanished, he jerked beneath her hand and a sound, something between a growl and a groan, erupted from his chest.

Then she was being swept up in the hard strength of his powerful arms and deposited in the middle of his bed. She lay, breathless and waiting as she watched him yank the shirt over his head, buttons popping.

He toed off his shoes. Undid his belt. His zipper

being lowered was the only sound in the room, then his trousers pooled at his feet and he stepped out of them. Naked with that magnificent erection jutting at her, he transformed from urban sophisticate to primeval man.

She was in awe. Aroused, yes. Apprehensive, definitely. But, watching his long thighs with their dusting of dark masculine hair flex as he climbed onto the bed with her, she was mostly in awe.

He straddled her, gripped her wrists, holding them above her head, and looked into her eyes. 'Leave your arms there,' he instructed. The only body parts touching were their hands and his knees against her hips. Then he slid to the bottom of the bed and pushed her thighs apart.

And the world ceased to exist.

Only the feel of his tongue, moist and warm, leaving a damp trail that cooled in the air as he worked his way from instep to ankle, to the inside of her knee. Higher...

She might have come right there, right then, but he only skimmed the place yearning for him most and moved on to suckle each of her nipples gently with teeth and lips and tongue, teasing them into stiff, aching peaks. And all the while his hands were moving, touching, exploring, fingers gliding up the inside of her arms to twine once more with hers.

That simple connection, the joining of hands as he looked into her eyes… She closed her eyes to block him out. No one had ever made love to her like this before. No one had ever made her feel this way before. But uncomplicated sex was all she was looking for, she told herself, and so was he—they'd both just admitted as much.

So she concentrated on his warm masculine scent, the friction of hot skin on hot skin. Every movement, every murmur, every breath, invoked a different sensation, a new experience in delight. She wanted to touch him the way he'd touched her, but the grip of his fingers held her fast.

Cameron didn't want to loosen his grip, even when he felt her resistance. 'Not yet,' he whispered against her ear.

He had her right where he wanted her, with her hard little nipples prodding his chest, her heart beating out the wild rhythm echoing his own. Somewhere in the back of his mind it mystified him that someone as individual as Didi, as opposed to him as north and south, should match him in any way.

She was all compact curves and sinuous limbs.

Fire roared through his veins, hammered in his groin. The urge to plunge into her wet heat without further preliminaries and satisfy himself slammed into him like a fully loaded cement truck on steroids. But he'd barely started. He wanted to see the passion build in those silver eyes, to watch her come undone beneath him—and he had to unlock their hands to do that.

He banked the fire, let it smoulder through his system. Slow. Freeing her to do her own exploring while taking her with him on his leisurely tour of discovery. As he brushed his lips over skin as smooth as satin—a cheek, a shoulder, the softer flesh of her neck, each with their own unique fragrance and texture.

She might be somewhat naïve but she wasn't shy—a surprise given her innocent pixie-like charms. He hadn't counted on the ability of those small deft fingers to fan the embers into a red-hot need with such swiftness.

Another surprise. He didn't *need* women, he enjoyed them. And when the enjoyment faded, so did the relationship. Only Kat had managed to inveigle her way beneath his defences. His hand tightened a little over Didi's breast. Never again.

What had happened with her ex-lover? he wondered, watching her eyes turn to pewter as her fingernails scraped over his nipples, a tease of pleasure, a hint of pain. He slammed the thought to the back of his mind. But he couldn't shake the uneasy, unfamiliar feeling it evoked. Jealousy? Hardly.

His fingers tightened again on her flesh and an overwhelming need to possess her *now* seized him, tossed him high where there was only heat and need and greed. Forget slow—skimming the dip of her belly, he plunged three fingers into her tight wet centre.

She arched into his hand, writhed against him, eyes glassy and unfocused. 'Yes!'

At her urgent demand, he levered himself up, swung a thigh over her hips, and, taking his weight on his hands, he looked down at the woman beneath him. My God, she looked beautiful in passion. 'Protection.'

Her mouth rounded into a soft 'Oh...' and she stared at him, her gaze sharpening. 'Yes-s-s...' She trailed off and their fast unsteady breaths mingling in the tight space between them were the only sounds in the room's silence. Her eyes widened. 'Don't tell me you haven't...'

'Of course I have.' He shifted slightly, pulled open a drawer in his night-stand and withdrew a foil packet.

'Of course you have.' A crisp edge to her tone—and her eyes—as she watched him rip the foil, roll on the condom. As if she thought he got laid by a different woman every night of the week.

'Didi.' Taking his weight on his hands again he positioned himself above her. 'It's you and me. *Only* you and me.' Terms and conditions yet to be negotiated.

He waited a beat, every muscle in his arms quivering, every pulse-point hammering. Saw her understanding and acknowledgement, then, with a groan that seemed to come from some uncharted place inside him, he entered her in one long deep thrust.

She was different, was all he could think as he began to move inside her. Hotter, faster, it swept him up until everything faded except her body clinging to his, the fragrance of her fresh-soaped skin, her wet tightness surrounding him, accepting him. Claiming him.

He felt her teeter on the brink then shudder, her inner muscles drawing him deeper, further, harder until he dived over the edge with her.

* * *

Hours later, as dawn painted the clouds purple and gold behind the skyscrapers, Cam watched Didi's gold lashes rest on her cheeks. Not only was she beautiful in passion, he thought, but also in repose. If he could take the image from his brain, scan it into his computer and have a master painter recreate it, it could hang in the most prestigious art galleries of the world.

He watched her sigh, then snuggle into the quilt, and a small smile touched her lips, as if she was dreaming happy dreams. At some point they'd climbed beneath the covers. The room was warm, he couldn't resist—he lowered the quilt so that they were both naked from the waist up and he could get a look at her breasts dusted in the new day's light. He couldn't resist some more and blew on them gently, making them pebble as he watched.

His sex stirred. He wanted her again, with dawn's light smattering pink into her silver eyes. She was the most responsive woman he'd ever had. Sure he'd had women who knew a few good tricks in the bedroom, but they'd performed them with the polished ease of practice. What Didi lacked in polish she more than made up for in a delightfully naïve spontaneity.

A glance at his bedside clock warned him it wasn't going to happen now. He was due at the office for an early meeting and before he left he wanted answers. She'd promised them this morning. Then they were going to have a discussion about what they expected from this new direction their relationship had taken. And it all had to happen before they could leave this room because her sister would be waiting.

He leaned over, brushing his lips over hers. 'Wake up, Didi.'

Didi drifted on a tide of contentment. As she surfaced contentment turned to wariness as a deep voice and memories of last night dragged her awake. She opened her eyes.

Cameron Black.

She'd spent the night in his bed.

And didn't her body know it? she thought as vaguely pleasant aches and twinges in various places made themselves known.

'Good morning,' he murmured.

Had she ever woken to a more mouth-watering sight than that of Cameron sporting nothing but morning stubble and a smile? 'Good morning.'

Morning. The feeling of well-being faded and tension grabbed at her belly. Their little whatever-it-was was over and now she'd have to live under his roof—and his gaze—and endure the consequences of what they'd done. And there was still the problem of Veronica.

Suddenly all too aware of her nakedness, she dragged the quilt up to her chin, then, shoving a hand through what must look like porcupine hair, she sat up. 'What time is it?'

'Six-thirty.' He played with the ends of her bed hair and there was a twinkle in his eye when he said, 'We have a few things to discuss, Fairy-bread.'

'I was going to get to that. *Fairy bread?*'

'You know, buttered and covered in sprinkles and cut into tri—'

'I know what it is—what I don't know is why you called me that.'

'Because it's pretty—' he kissed her nose '—it tastes sweet—' he moved lower to nuzzle her neck '—and it was the best I could think of at short notice. We need to get our story straight before we face the dragon lady.'

She saw his amusement sober as he shifted away creating a space between them, but her mouth was dry and she needed a moment to gather her thoughts. 'Any chance of a coffee?'

'No. For all we know, your sister could be prowling the apartment looking for evidence to put me away.'

'More like she wants to catch *me* out,' Didi said. 'She knows this isn't real.'

His brows rose and something intimate crossed his expression. 'After that performance last night?'

Her cheeks heated. That was just it—it was only a performance. As for the rest...how he'd taken her to heights she'd never been...she couldn't think about that now.

'Why would she want to catch you out, Didi?' he asked quietly.

'My family...' She steepled her hands at her lips. She wished she could put on a robe, anything to cover her vulnerability, but she couldn't bring herself to climb out of bed naked. 'My parents are...well off, my older sister's married to a...' *pompous ass* '...wealthy owner of a string of luxury yachts.

'I never fitted in. You've seen my sister—tall, elegant, poised, sophisticated. Like my parents. They despaired of me right from the start. They wanted me to take piano lessons and study multiple languages. I wanted to use Mum's silk brocade curtains to make clothes, learn origami and study art.

'When I finished school I spent a couple of years overseas. But when I came back my parents said if I didn't go to uni I was on my own. So I found a boarding house on the cheap side of the city and got a job in a café. I took casual employment for the next couple of years, including stocking supermarket shelves and kitchen hand.'

'And somewhere along the way you met this guy who messed you up.'

She sighed, staring at the ceiling. 'I thought he was serious. Turned out there was someone else—*that there'd always been* that someone else. Which is why I don't want a serious relationship ever again.'

There had been too many painful memories of her broken heart and humiliation in Sydney. 'I decided to come to Melbourne to make a fresh start, so I told my parents I'd got a job in an exclusive gallery with a luxury apartment to boot.'

His chest hair rasped against her shoulder as he slid an arm around her in wordless support.

'She's just come to gloat. I couldn't let her. I

just couldn't. Not when I saw an opportunity. I'm sorry I went behind your back.'

He dropped a kiss on her head. 'I've got a strong back. How do you want to play it today?'

'Keep up the charade that we're...involved—'

'Lovers,' he reminded her. 'And it's not a charade. Not any more.'

'Until she leaves this afternoon,' she finished, her cheeks heating as her body reminded her in all kinds of ways of the fact that, no, it hadn't been a charade.

She felt him shift again, then he tilted her face to his. In his eyes something flickered and sent her pulse scrambling. 'Didi, how do you feel about extending this arrangement a little longer? Say, two and a half weeks?'

'What do you mean?' She tried to keep her voice even, her expression neutral.

But she knew what he meant and blood pounded through her veins. A ball of fire lodged behind her breastbone, shooting flares up and down the length of her body.

He wanted her, here. In this bed. And she didn't need rocket science to work it out.

If she wanted, for two and a half weeks she could be Cameron Black's live-in mistress.

CHAPTER EIGHT

DIDI backed up on the mattress towards the edge of the bed, holding the sheet in front of her breasts, her gaze scouring the room. Better, she thought, to look for something to cover herself than to look him in the eye because one glance at her response and he'd know the effect he'd had on her. And that would be a distinct disadvantage.

So he'd used the word 'lover' in this morning's conversation—now he was suggesting an 'arrangement'. And suggesting amazingly coolly for something as hot as an affair with Cameron Black would be. Too coolly. As if he were negotiating one of his property deals.

'You know exactly what I mean,' he murmured. 'What do you say?' His tone told her he expected an affirmative answer.

And how easy would it be—mistress to a millionaire, a heap of money in commissions? She'd walk away richer at the end. Ah, but would she still be happy when she walked away? Better, safer, to stick to their original agreement.

'I...don't think so,' she said. Pleased with how calm she sounded even if she was coming apart inside, still avoiding eye contact. Still feeling vulnerable. 'Um...do you have a bathrobe I can put on?'

With that same cool confidence he padded naked to the bathroom, plucked a terry robe from behind the door. Ah, and she couldn't help but look, could she? But it didn't seem to faze him— nor the fact that he was in a state of semi-arousal. No, well, it was that male pride thing, obviously.

He tossed her the robe on his way back and retrieved last night's discarded trousers from the floor. He didn't bother with underwear. He came around to her side of the bed. Her body hummed as remnants of last night's electricity arced between them. Then he ran a thumb over her lower lip. 'So...you don't think so, huh?'

She jerked as if that electricity had zapped her. 'I told you last night, I don't like your type.' To put on the robe she had to let go of the sheet... She closed her eyes so she couldn't see him watching her and slipped her arms inside. Rising, she moved to the window and watched the morning traffic build.

'No,' he said behind her. 'Last night you said you didn't like *me*. There's a difference. Tell me more about my *type*.'

'I've told you before...' She trailed off as she tightened the sash, aware of the robe's familiar soap scent enveloping her. Cameron's scent.

Her opinion of the type of man he was *had* changed since that first night. She'd seen a different side of him: a caring, thoughtful man who'd trusted her with a large sum of cash and allowed her to stay in his apartment—and look what she'd done to repay him. She'd brought in an uninvited guest last night and she'd barely scratched the canvas she'd promised she'd start.

Still, she didn't have to like him on principle, she decided, hugging her arms around her. With his million-dollar lifestyle and Italian-made suits. She might have had a similar upbringing but she'd always been aware of the poverty never far from her door.

It was a long way from his.

She'd decided it was easier and less complicated to *not* like him...except now it was too late for

easy and it had just got a whole lot more complicated.

She'd had sex with him.

'Didi,' he said behind her. 'Regardless of my *type,* why stop at one night when there's clearly a chemistry between us we could explore further?'

She could feel that simmering chemistry from half a dozen steps away. How could he feel so hot yet sound so cool? Nor did she need any further investigation. She already knew his was the kind of love-making that burned all the way through and left a brand on your heart and a glow on your skin.

Only if you let it.

'As I said last night we have a working rela-tionship,' she said. 'And in three weeks we won't even have that.'

'So we lay some ground rules.' He planted an open-mouthed kiss on the back of her neck. An-other on the soft flesh between neck and shoul-der. Then steadied her with his hands as he turned her to face him.

'Ground rules...?' Her heart was pumping so hard she wondered it didn't explode out of her chest.

'You work here during the day and I work at the office.'

'And nights...?'

'We explore what we have in common.' The glitter in his eyes didn't need clarification. It was all about the sex and they both knew it.

'And when the time's up I walk away, no complications on either side.'

'Exactly.'

Like a business transaction. 'That's plain enough.' She stepped away from him again and began picking up her clothes from where she'd dropped them at the bottom of the bed last night.

What did she expect? She'd flirted with him, pushed his buttons, got him to play along with this crazy idea of convincing her sister he was her lover.

'You don't seem too thrilled about it.'

She flashed him a glare over her shoulder as she picked her T-shirt up off the floor. 'Should I be?'

'You liked it well enough last night. Didi.' His voice softened. 'What happened with your last guy won't happen with us because we both know up front what we're getting into. So long as we have mutual respect and understanding.'

She straightened and forced herself to look at him.

'And I'll include other benefits, of course.'

'Other benefits?'

'I attend a lot of charity events; some are quite formal affairs where a partner is expected. If we go out in the evening, I'll pay any expenses, clothes, salon procedures et cetera.'

'You mean you want me to accompany you? To functions where you're exhibiting your next property development?' She scoffed. 'Like, I'm on the other side of the fence—how could I do *that* with a clear conscience?'

A look she couldn't interpret crossed his face. 'You're not as far away from my side as you think, Didi.' He scratched his chin. 'The alternative would be for me to chaperone some other woman and I don't think that arrangement would work.'

The thought of him with *some other woman* while she sat in his apartment working her fingers to the bone poured acid on her empty stomach, but she remembered, 'Did you forget I may need to work through evenings?'

He shook his head. 'Not every evening, Didi. You'll need some down-time. I'm the last person who'd want to compromise your creativity. And

I'll ensure it's not something you wouldn't feel comfortable attending before I accept.'

She couldn't look at him while she made her decision so she studied the pile of clothes in her hand. She'd have to be very, very careful not to let herself fall for him. Because she would *not* go through that kind of pain again.

She had to remember to keep her heart out of the mix. Keep it temporary. Casual sex. Except she'd never done casual sex.

But she knew this inexplicable attraction was mutual and she wanted to explore that attraction while she was here. And, damn it, why shouldn't she? They were both single, unattached and available and this was twenty-first-century Australia.

Finally, she met his gaze. 'I'll be wearing my own clothes if we go out, thanks. And believe it when I tell you no one can manage my hair but me.'

Cam let out a deep slow breath as he watched Didi run her hands through the unruly tufts. He hadn't realised he'd been holding his breath and mentally shook his head at the sheer madness of whatever-the-hell-it-was that had gripped him until he saw the agreement in her eyes.

Sex was the motivation, right? Yet this crazy

feeling was like nothing he'd ever felt before. Before he could stop himself he crossed the room to take that beautiful bewitching face between his hands and watch last night's afterglow in her eyes sparkle.

She smelled of sleep and sex and his mouth fell onto hers as if he'd relinquished control of his movements to some unseen force. Unthinkable to resist. Impossible to pretend he wasn't instantly aroused by her warm womanly shape beneath the terry-towelling robe, by the feel of her hands sliding around his naked back as she fashioned herself against him.

Exclusively his for the next two and a half weeks.

The sound of someone passing by the door pulled him out of the moment. Reluctant, he drew back, soothing her lips with his before he said, 'I'd better make myself presentable while you go see if our guest wants some breakfast.' *And I need to put some priorities in order, starting now.*

'Hmm.' Her fingers found their way beneath his waistband and she looked up at him. 'I kind of like you unpresentable.'

Drawing her hands away, he clasped them together. 'Go. Now. Before I forget I'm supposed to be the host.' *And that today's another business day with a couple of site inspections and three meetings scheduled.*

Twenty minutes later he helped himself to a mug of coffee. Veronica was sipping from her own mug on the sofa by the living-room window while Didi took eggs from the refrigerator. The apartment's open-plan living arrangement allowed him to view both women simultaneously.

Two sisters couldn't be more different. It wasn't lost on him that at a purely superficial level Veronica was more like the usual type of woman who shared the occasional breakfast here before they went their separate ways to work.

Charlie greeted Cam as he carried his steaming mug towards the sofa. Why was it that cats invariably chose to smooch people who ignored them? But he bent down to fondle the silky ears as he nodded at their guest. 'Veronica. I apologise for not being up earlier. I trust you slept well?'

'I did. Thank you.' Sipping delicately, she eyed him with a hint of the distrust she'd shown last night. 'You have a lovely apartment.'

'We like it.' He smiled at Didi, who was whipping up eggs with one eye and watching them with another.

Veronica arched a brow. 'How long have you been here, Didi?'

The whisk faltered but only for a second. 'Um... not long...'

'Didi's a relative newcomer but I've been here a few years.' Cam covered the hitch smoothly.

'Ah...' Veronica eyed him with an I-know-your-game glint and when she spoke her voice was silk. 'You're the gallery owner who leases it to my sister for a low rent. How...convenient. But you're not interstate—Didi told me you were.'

He glanced at Didi, back to Veronica. 'And so I was...yesterday.'

Glancing at the Sheila Dodd and Didi's work against the wall, she observed, 'You're also an art collector.'

'Actually, the Before the Temptation one is mine,' Didi said, setting two frying pans on the stove with satisfied clangs. 'Scrambled eggs okay?'

'Yes. Fine.' Veronica paused, sculptured brows rising. 'Yours?'

'Yep. As in I made it.'

'Beautifully crafted, isn't it?' Cam said, smiling, watching Veronica's bemused expression. 'It should fetch a tidy price at the gallery.'

'It's not for sale,' Didi said over the counter top.

'Ah...yes. Very nice.' Veronica set her mug down with a delicate clink. No well-deserved praise, Cam noted.

'Mum and Dad send their love.' Casually spoken but Cam felt the immediate undercurrent between the two sisters.

Wouldn't they have had this conversation yesterday? This was purely for his benefit.

Didi only glanced up as she stirred eggs into one pan, set bacon sizzling in the other. 'I've been very busy.'

'Too busy to call?'

Silence except for the crackle of bacon. 'I'll do things my way, Veronica,' Didi said finally. 'When I'm ready.' She sliced avocado onto plates.

Cam watched the interaction. Clearly Didi had further issues with her parents that she'd yet to share with him.

'So where did you two meet?'

Didi caught Cam's eye, then said, 'At a cocktail party.'

He grinned back at Didi over his coffee. 'I turned around and there she was. It was literally sparks at three paces.'

'Really? So, Cameron, this gallery you own...'

Her pursed lips were quite deliberate. 'That makes you Didi's boss?'

'Not exactly. Didi's working on a commission at present,' Cam said carefully. 'Her work's going to be demanding a small fortune soon.' No lies there. 'You'll have to put in an order before word gets out.'

'It's not really my thing,' Veronica said with a lazy disinterest that annoyed Cam. 'Fabric and threads collect dust. Daniel's allergies wouldn't allow it.'

How could she be so dismissive of her sister's talent? 'Unfortunate,' was all Cam allowed himself to say but he felt his hackles rise on Didi's account. He suppressed the urge to slice into Veronica. 'Smells like breakfast's ready. Shall we adjourn to the breakfast bar?'

Veronica left a short time later with Cameron's limo made available until her flight departed. As Didi cleared the dishes into the dishwasher she turned to see that her lover had disappeared behind a neatly pressed businessman with money-making on his agenda. He was studying her work-in-progress—or lack of—with a calculating eye.

Tension gripped the base of her skull but she refused to let his authoritarian stance intimidate her, or the fact that they'd spent the night naked together prevent her from saying, 'I spent yesterday sketching designs and collecting supplies.'

'What have you decided on?' he asked, flipping through her boxes of threads and silks.

'This one.' She handed him the outline she'd decided on. 'I thought fire. It's fluid and alive; a rising-from-the-ashes kind of thing. Contrasts—obscurity and brilliance.'

'The eternal flame,' Cameron mused. 'A memorial. Appropriate.' He paced to the window, hands in his pockets, stared out for a long moment before turning to her. 'You have everything you need?'

'For now, yes. A memorial to whom?'

An expression of barely veiled regret crossed his face before he blinked it away and a wistfulness crept into his eyes, a small smile tipped his mouth. 'Someone I knew. Someone I owe.'

Who had he known? Who did he owe? Why didn't he tell her?

Because this arrangement was only temporary, she reminded herself. She didn't need to know his life history. And this was the right choice of theme, she thought, watching him. This was the emotion she wanted to capture—darkness into light—and it obviously resonated with him.

He seemed to shake away whatever it was that put the shadows in his eyes. 'I'll see you this evening, then.' He spoke briskly as he crossed the room to pick up his briefcase from beside the sofa.

Not a hint of the man who'd practically worshipped her body last night with hands and mouth and…more. He could have been talking to anyone. The only concession he made was a chaste almost impersonal kiss on her cheek. 'Have a productive day.'

She was tempted to throw her arms around his neck and demand something of last night's passion but she kept her hands at her sides, remembered their deal and said, 'You too.'

He didn't even give her time to see if a remnant of the night's heat lingered in his eyes because he was already walking away, leaving a souvenir of his scent on the air.

She stood watching the elevator doors long after they'd closed. Long after she'd heard its muted hum as it took him away to his world of wheeling and dealing and knocking down buildings.

Didi forced the hot memories to the back of her mind the way he obviously had. *Think business arrangement.* For Cameron there was no blurring of lines. She needed to do the same. Keep it in perspective. In three weeks their *business* would be concluded.

Didi did her best work to music so she chose one of her own CDs and slid it into Cameron's sound system, cranked up the volume. Ravel's 'Bolero' throbbed out of the speakers, eerie, edgy.

She closed her eyes a few moments, absorbed its building passion, the throbbing swirl of emotion. Not until she'd visualised the finished work did she slip on her glasses and begin.

Hours passed. Hunger was forgotten, cramped muscles ignored, aching fingers disregarded. She worked until the surrounding buildings' lengthening shadows slid through the windows and the sky grew scarlet behind the silhouette of the Rialto Towers, turning the Yarra River to blood.

It took a few moments to emerge from her labours. Placing her glasses on the table, she stood back to study the day's work with a critical eye. Nothing much to see yet, but she'd made a start on the foundation.

Stretching, rolling tense shoulders, she moved to the window and watched the city's lights appear in a rainbow of colours. That tension at the base of her skull was back, a dull echo to her heartbeat, and her eyes felt gritty. It occurred to her that she had no idea what time Cameron would be home.

The thought of seeing him again sent a wave of excitement through her, and a rising panic. Did he expect her to dress up for him? Or dress 'down'— as in gauzy negligee with a welcome-home glass of champagne in her hand? Did the 'evening' part of their arrangement begin at sunset? Or did it only exist between the sheets?

When did his employee transform into his magical mistress?

She scoffed at her new persona, but her laugh caught in her throat when she stepped into the bedroom. The unmade bed, with its sheets wrinkled and quilt dragging on the thick carpet, was a testament to their torrid night. Was making beds a part of her job description now? Which had her wondering, did Cameron carry out those domestic tasks himself or did he have a regular cleaning service?

The phone on the night-stand shrilled. 'Hello?' As had happened yesterday, whoever it was disconnected without speaking. She stared at the receiver while a sick feeling of betrayal rose up inside her, throbbing in time with the pulse in her head. A woman, she was sure of it.

His ex that maybe wasn't an ex any more?

She shook her head. Just because Jay had gone back to his ex-lover didn't mean Cameron would. It was paranoia making her think that way. But it *was* a timely reminder of the temporary nature of their relationship.

She picked up her towelling robe from the bed, determined to put the incident out of her mind. She needed to stretch out the kinks with a long, fragrant soak in that guest bathroom's spa before she felt even human again, let alone magical.

And as for dressing up—or down—it wasn't an option. Either he accepted her somewhat offbeat and eclectic style or he didn't. She no longer had the luxury of money to waste on frivolous dresses or seduce-me nightgowns, nor did she feel a need to conform to the gurus of fashion.

And if she didn't do something about this developing migraine, she thought as she rummaged in her bag for medication, she'd be no use to anyone, including herself.

She stripped off, shrugged into the robe's comforting warmth, sat on the edge of the bed. Tempting to lay her head on the pillow—the one that smelled of him—just for a moment. Then she'd have that soak and then...

CHAPTER NINE

CAM closed his folder and glanced at his watch as the last of the attendees exited the room. The meeting had run late. He'd been running late since he arrived this morning.

It didn't usually bother him—he practically lived at the office, often making up for lost time well after midnight when necessary. Tonight wasn't one of those nights. Tonight anticipation snapped at his heels and he couldn't wait to be out the door.

That brought him up short. *Slow down, Cam.* It wasn't as if he needed to see *her,* he assured himself. He didn't *need* anyone. Need threatened control, something he'd fought for most of his life, and won.

So he sent his driver home and set out to walk the forty minutes to his apartment. He deliberately took his time, strolling along tree-lined Collins Street where spring was showing itself with tiny green buds gleaming in the street lights. Ducking rattling trams and harried pedestrians at one of the busy intersections. Workers were cramming cafés for an early dinner, hitting the city gyms or shopping. The smell of fast food mingled with car exhaust fumes.

He found his pace picking up and slowed once more. Didi was in his head again, and too much for his peace of mind. He wanted to see how the work was coming along, the artist herself was a… fringe benefit. A diversion.

Yet even as he told himself that was all it was he knew he was fooling himself. Didi O'Flanagan was one hell of a diversion…and a whole lot more. The fact that they clashed on so many points only added to the appeal.

And the sex was… More. It was the only description he could come up with.

He found himself outside his apartment building and rode the elevator up. He'd been surprised to learn she came from wealth; she clearly championed for the disadvantaged. Why would her parents have nothing to do with her? There was obviously more to it than she was willing to let him see. A woman with secrets—a good reason not to trust her too easily.

The apartment was silent when he stepped inside. Charlie trotted towards him, twining himself around his legs, a furry ribbon with an appetite. Priorities, he reminded himself. He went to the living room to view the work-in-progress. Not much to see yet, but she'd been busy. Her glasses lay amongst the scatter. He fed the cat. So, now… where was Didi—and what was she doing?

His pulse rate accelerated as he headed for his bedroom and his steps quickened. As he stepped inside the spill of low light from the bedside lamp highlighted her face, glinted on her hair. Fast asleep, her complexion pale, smudges beneath her eyes.

Then his gaze fell on a bottle of pills on the night-stand. Gut-curdling dread clawed its way up his throat, choking off his air. Visions from the past flashed before his eyes. Amy had done this to herself on a regular basis. His mother had died of an overdose of prescription drugs.

He grabbed the bottle as he shook her shoulder with rough impatience. 'Didi.' *For God's sake.* 'Wake up!' Belatedly a glance at the bottle informed him they were prescription pills for migraine.

She stirred. 'Huh? What?' He saw her wince

as she opened her eyes, squinting in the glare. 'What is it?'

He blew out a slow breath. 'I'm sorry. I shouldn't have woken you. I just...' He noted his hand wasn't steady as he brushed hair from her brow. 'Go back to sleep.'

She blinked up at him as her eyes adjusted to the light. 'I was going to take a dip in that swimming-pool spa of yours. I guess I zonked out.'

'Do you still have your headache?' He cleared the residual panic from his throat and let his hand rest on her shoulder. She felt warm, soft. Alive.

'No.' She sounded surprised and rubbed her brow, checking. 'No.'

'Lie there for a bit. I have to go out for a while. Do you think you'll feel like eating later? I can bring something back if you want.'

She rolled onto her side, the robe dipping and slipping, tempting his own appetite with generous slices of cleavage and thigh. She moistened her lips, drawing his gaze. 'Why do you have to go out? Friday night's for relaxing. Stay.'

He doubted she knew how husky she sounded, how provocative she looked, drowsy from sleep and sexy as sin. The whole effect shook him to his foundations and, coupled with the near heart attack she'd just given him, he was in no mood to analyse his angry response, nor why he felt the need to distance himself.

He rose. 'I have a standing appointment on Friday evenings and I don't intend to break it. Not even for you.' In three weeks she'd be gone, a pleasant memory.

Her expression cooled. 'This *arrangement* we have—I thought it was exclusive.'

'It is.' He turned away, strode to his wardrobe.

Didi flopped onto her back and stared at the ceiling, unaccountably hurt, unreasonably disappointed. Why was she feeling this way? Because the memory of that earlier mystery phone call hammered at her and it was all too easy to draw her own conclusions. 'I'm not going to sit here and wait for you every night,' she said, listening to the rustle of clothes on the other side of the partially open door.

She could almost hear his eyes rolling back in his head as he said, 'It's not every night, Didi, it's Friday nights.'

He strode back into the room and every accusation—every thought—dried on her tongue.

He was wearing jeans. Blue jeans. Faded, scruffy, worn jeans with a T-shirt that had been black once, and two sizes too small because it stretched over his chest like elastic over the Harbour Bridge.

And she'd thought he looked sexy in a business suit… She'd thought he couldn't look more sexy, but he did, in a dangerous, bad-boy way that called to the wanton woman inside her.

And he was going out. Without her.

She so didn't care. She wished she had a nail file and polish handy, or a magazine so she could flick through the pages ever so carelessly and show him just how much she so didn't care. Instead she shrugged. 'Slumming it tonight, huh?'

He stilled, every hard ripple in that impressive chest tense, every muscle in his jaw bunched. His lips compressed into a tight angry line. Something dangerous flashed in his eyes—not in that bad-boy way, but in a way that made her want to shrink back and wish the sarcastic words unsaid. Definitely the lowest form of wit.

'Get dressed,' he said calmly. Too calmly. 'You want to see slumming? Come with me. Be ready in five minutes. I can't be late. I *won't* be late. Wear comfortable shoes and bring a jacket.'

There was no thought of refusal. Her fingers trembled as she dragged on jeans and a jumper she found amongst her stuff. This showed a side of Cameron she'd never seen, never known existed. A quick glance in the mirror reflected a face devoid of make-up, hollows beneath her eyes. She spiked her hair with her fingers—that would have to do. She dragged out her worn coat, slipped it on.

They rode the elevator down to the underground car park in silence, climbed into the car and merged into the evening traffic the same way. Considering the dress code it was almost absurd to be driving in such luxury with something classically high-brow playing through the speakers.

Whatever it was, this was very important to Cameron, and it would give her some insight into the man who didn't talk about himself.

Fitzroy's busy inner suburban street was crammed with traffic, tram lines and overhanging cables, some of the beautiful architecture of a bygone era mottled with peeling paint, boarded up or covered in graffiti. Light years away from Cameron's exclusive Collins Street address. He parked in a side street.

'You're leaving this expensive piece of automotive engineering here?' she said, incredulous.

'It's only a car, Didi.'

She bit back a retort that only an hour ago she wouldn't have hesitated to use and climbed out.

It became obvious he was heading for what had once been an old department store. The tired red bricks on the second and third storey remained but the street-level façade had been given fresh paint and the windows at the front were large and brightly lit. Inviting. The sign read, 'Come In Centre'.

She saw a medical clinic, still open. Lights spilled from the room Cameron explained was a youth counselling service. The atmosphere was vibrant and alive, busy. She followed him through a large recreational room where people, mostly teenagers, watched TV, played table tennis, or sat at tables talking.

She could smell unwashed bodies, poverty, fear, but she also sensed optimism and hope and determination.

'This building's for abused teenagers and runaways,' he said as they made their way through the high-ceilinged room towards a canteen. 'Here they can get a meal, see a doctor, talk with professionals who care, and generally hang out.'

'You did this.' Didi looked up at him with newfound respect, but his eyes were an unforgiving navy steel. 'You renovated this building. You financed it yourself.'

His shoulders tensed, he put his hands in the back pockets of his jeans and kept walking. 'It doesn't happen on its own.'

'Stop.' She caught his arm, felt the resistance beneath her fingers. He didn't want to be touched, but she needed the contact. Needed to say, 'Hang on a minute. I'm sorry I said what I said back at the apartment. I'm sorry for a lot of things I've said to you,' she finished quietly.

The steel in his eyes didn't soften. If it was possible, they hardened. 'You couldn't begin to understand the meaning of destitute. You *chose* the way you currently live your life. You *chose* to leave your family. These kids don't have that luxury.'

She knew. It made her feel ashamed. But Cameron... 'Why did you do it? Why are you involved?'

Shadows flitted over his gaze but he shook his head and kept walking.

They reached the restaurant-sized kitchen where a round woman with flyaway brown hair and two double chins was dishing greens and mash and some sort of spicy-smelling stew onto plates for the kids lined up at the counter.

'Ah, Cameron, right on time.' The woman smiled at them over her ladle. 'And you've brought us a new assistant. Good, because we're really busy tonight. Sandra couldn't make it.'

'Hello, Joan. This is Didi,' he said, walking behind the counter. He tossed Didi an apron. 'Let's get started, then. Joan'll fill you in on what needs to be done. I'll be back in a few moments.'

'Welcome, Didi.' She smiled with genuine warmth, brown eyes twinkling. 'I hope you're wearing comfortable shoes.' Joan glanced at Didi's sneakers, filled another plate. 'Cameron's never brought a girlfriend here before.'

Didi felt her cheeks warm. 'I'm not his girlfriend.' *Just his temporary mistress.* 'I'm working on an arts project for him.'

'And supporting him in your free time, good for you. There's not many willing to put in the effort on a Friday night.' She pulled loaves of bread from the shelf behind them, set them in front of Didi. 'You can start on the sandwiches. You'll find everything you need in the fridge. You'll need a knife.' She handed her a key, gestured to a drawer. 'We keep them locked away—one never knows...'

They worked side by side, ladling stew and cutting sandwiches.

'*You're* working here on a Friday night,' Didi prompted after a few moments. 'Do you help out often?'

'Every week. Cameron looked out for my son when he turned up here lost and alone. Thanks to him, my abusive ex is locked up and I have my son back.' She flicked hair off her face with the back of her hand. 'I don't know where these kids would be without him.'

Every so often Didi saw Cameron walk through the canteen, talking to kids. Holding a hand, squeezing a shoulder. Listening. Caring.

Who was this man? She'd mentally accused him of not wanting to soil his suit yet here he was, hands-on and involved. Again, why? In the short time they'd known each other he'd not spoken of family and she hadn't asked. What was the point? It wasn't as if he were going to introduce her, nor did she want to meet them. Their relationship wasn't the kind that involved family.

Shaking off the hollow feeling, she plastered ham and tomato onto buttered bread. She didn't want to dissect her emotions because right now they were too close to the surface and too vulnerable. If she let him, he could steal her heart and leave her dead inside.

No. Once was more than enough. But now, as he leaned over a table to speak with a couple of boys in their late teens she couldn't seem to take her eyes off him.

She tried observing him from a purely feminine viewpoint without the tug of emotion. Below the T-shirt's short sleeves, the hard definition of his arms, olive-skinned and dusted with dark hair. The innate strength in that upper body. The way his jeans hugged his tight backside, the faded denim down the front of his thighs and where the zipper chafed...

I know what's inside those jeans.

The recent memory of his body over hers—inside hers—speared through her and the knife she held slipped on the tomato she was holding. Which was okay, she told herself. It was a purely sexual zing—no emotions hence no vulnerability.

Until he glanced over as if he'd known she was watching and their gazes locked. Intense cobalt eyes studied her. Even from across the room she felt the heat all the way down to her toes. *Sexual attraction,* she assured herself. Tonight they'd act on that attraction. Again. Another zing hummed through her like an electrical jolt. Anticipation.

But the sound of voices, the smell of food and kids, faded. The whole scene blurred around the edges. Only Cameron remained in focus, as if she were looking through a tunnel. She saw his fingers tighten on the edge of the table. His jaw tightened infinitesimally. He didn't straighten but she knew the muscles in his back had turned rigid.

She knew because it was happening to her.

His eyes relayed a message she didn't want to read—emotion. She felt her own emotions flow to him on a tide of something perilously close to trust.

Vulnerability.

No. Dragging her eyes away, she concentrated on loosening her grip on the knife, rolled tension from her shoulders. *That* wasn't supposed to happen. Wasn't going to happen. Not even when she noticed he was making his way towards her, still watching her with those bluer-than-blue eyes.

'Not your boyfriend, eh?' Joan chuckled. 'He's been distracted all evening. And you too, I think.'

Didi glared at the sandwich as she sliced it into ruthless triangles, *not* being distracted by the man and her unwise reaction to him. 'I don't need a man in my life.'

'Ah, but maybe he needs you,' Joan murmured.

Didi's laugh came too fast, sounded too brittle. She reached for more bread, more ham. Cameron's 'need' for Didi wasn't the kind Joan was referring to. It would never be anything else. *Cameron* had made it quite clear their three-week arrangement was all there was.

And she'd agreed.

So...maybe that made it okay to watch him as a purely sexual being... She lifted her eyes... He was talking to a boy with a baseball cap on backwards and dirt-stained hands.

A shout nearby had Didi turning sharply. A teenager had collapsed and was lying on the floor. Cameron was beside the girl in seconds. 'Call an ambulance!' he yelled as pandemonium broke out amongst the crowd gathering around the unconscious girl. 'Everyone move back. Joey, go wait out the front for the ambos.'

Joan flew into action, phoning the emergency services while Didi rushed around the counter and elbowed her way to Cameron's side. 'Anything I can do?' Didi's heart was thumping. The girl was sheet white, her lips blue, skin cold to the touch when Didi took her hand.

'Stay out of the way.' His attention didn't waver as Didi chafed the girl's hand and kids jostled for a better look.

'And get those kids back,' he barked. 'She's unresponsive, barely breathing.' He shoved up her sleeve, revealing the tell-tale bruising. 'Overdose.' He expelled a four-letter word, then muttered, 'Lizzie, when are you going to learn?'

He knew her name, Didi thought. He knew the kids' names. Didi absorbed that information for a split second, then, snapping into action, she shooed the audience back, giving Cameron air and space to work.

He checked the patient again. 'Mask.' His voice snapped with authority—no nerves, just an iron control—obviously he'd done this before, and more than once.

Joan appeared, dropping to her knees beside him, handing him the requested mask. He placed it over the girl's mouth and nose and immediately began resuscitation.

Seconds dragged by without end. Cameron worked steadily, breathing for the girl while Joan checked her pulse and Didi kept a clear space between them and the onlookers.

Finally, finally, the wail of a siren. Chaos, noise as paramedics rushed in with equipment. Pressing her lips together to bring the circulation back, Didi turned away. She couldn't look at Cameron right now. Black spots danced in front of her own eyes. Blame her earlier migraine and medication and lack of food, but, damn, she would *not* pass out in front of him.

She knew now why he'd been so panicked when he woke her earlier. She'd left her pills on the night-stand, he'd jumped to conclusions. And little wonder. She sank onto the nearest chair.

A few moments later she heard the wail of the sirens fade as the ambulance sped away, the background noise of voices and chairs scraping and the drum of her own heartbeat.

She didn't know how long she sat there. She knew Cameron and Joan were busy, calming kids, talking to those who'd been with Lizzie. Making phone calls.

'You okay?' Cameron sat down at the table opposite her, his warm steady hand enveloped her own and dark eyes met hers. Sweat dotted his brow. The lines around his mouth looked deeper. He'd probably been on the go all day and then this…and now her. 'Yes. Is…she going to be all right?'

The worry lines etched deeper into his brow. 'We've done what we can, now we wait. I'll phone the hospital later.'

'You were brilliant back there.'

He shook his head. 'You look beat. Let's get you out of here.'

She squared her shoulders and sat straighter. 'I might look a little under the weather tonight, but I'm not the fragile woman you think I am. I've worked in drop-in centres like this in Sydney. I've seen it before.'

She saw a new respect in his eyes but he only said, 'You were ill this afternoon.'

'I'm fine now. I can wait if you're not done.'

'I was on my way over to tell you we were leaving.'

'I need to help Joan clean—'

'She's got it covered. We're closing up now.'

Didi noticed the kids dispersing. A security guard manned the door. 'Where will they go now?'

'Wherever they came from.' He blew out a

breath. 'At least they know they'll be safe here, if only for a little while. Come on.'

'They trust you,' Didi murmured. And trust, not the sexual buzz she got from his touch, had her putting her hand in his when he offered it over the table top.

CHAPTER TEN

CAM parked the car in the basement. He must be mad—a willing woman waiting to warm his bed and blot out the memories that stalked him tonight more than most, and he was hesitating.

The tension in the car had been building all the way home. He'd blanked out the past hour's events and concentrated on nothing except how quickly he could get Didi naked. A survival mechanism, he supposed.

Now he burned, his groin hardening to her proximity, her subtle soap scent teasing his nostrils. He could be inside her slick wet heat in under five minutes, filling his hands with silky flesh and familiarising himself with her taste in all those musky feminine places he'd not explored to his satisfaction yet.

Blocking out the bad.

So why was he gripping the steering wheel and saying, 'How about a stroll?'

She turned to him, her eyes unreadable. 'If you want.'

But he couldn't interpret that tone of voice as he watched her push open the door. He'd made a mistake taking her there tonight, he thought now, grabbing a jacket from the back seat. Allowing her to see more of him than he'd intended.

He pressed his keypad, the click of the locks echoed in the car park's stillness, then he turned to Didi. Her skin appeared almost translucent under the harsh fluorescent light and he hesitated. 'You sure you're up to it?'

She wrapped her coat tighter about her. 'Of course I am.'

They walked a few moments, not touching. They crossed Flinders Street and took the pedestrian bridge over the River Yarra to Southbank. The night breeze carried the smell of the river. An enticing aroma of Japanese cooking. He could hear the ebb and flow of voices and a band playing a nightspot nearby. If he looked up, the Eureka Tower blotted out the stars. If only he could blot out the past as easily.

His mouth was dry; he longed for a double whisky on ice. Something to dull the edge. 'I could do with a drink. There's a bar I think you'll like.' He took her hand in his.

Polished auburn marble spread warmth throughout the lobby, shards of light refracted rainbows from the huge chandeliers.

'We're not dressed for this place,' Didi said as they passed function attendees in glittering gowns and crisp dinner suits making their way down the wide curving staircase. 'It's five star, for goodness' sake.'

'You should feel right at home, then.' Realising sarcasm was inappropriate, he squeezed her fingers. 'No one's looking at us.'

It occurred to him that Kat wouldn't be seen dead in worn jeans in a place like this. Kat wouldn't be seen in worn jeans, period, nor had she ever accompanied him to the drop-in centre. Whereas Didi had apparently been involved in a similar voluntary capacity.

He found a spot in the lounge bar, relatively private, overlooking the lobby where water rippled over marble and ornate gilt mirrors reflected elaborate floral arrangements on glass-topped tables.

'What would you like?'

She shook her head as she removed her coat.

'Nothing alcoholic; I took that medication earlier. A pot of green tea if they serve it.'

'Tea, it is.'

She folded her arms, rested them on the table, her shadowed cleavage above a faded pink T-shirt a temptation to forget about Lizzie and Amy and the whole damn world and concentrate on the sweet diversion she could offer.

When the world went crazy... 'Aside from the tea what would you really like?'

Her eyes sparkled in the lights. 'To be able to snuggle back into my dressing gown on a couch deep enough to get lost in and...' She trailed off, her voice husky with memories of last night as her eyes met his. And the sparkle turned hot.

He allowed the unspoken to smoulder a moment. 'Forget the dressing gown and tell me the rest.'

Her cheeks turned pink. 'You've got other things on your mind. I—'

'Damn right, I've got things on my mind. Starting with you, Didi...'

Their order arrived and the words hung between them with all their erotic possibilities. Ice clinked, china rattled as the waiter set the tea and a tumbler of whisky over ice on the table. Cam paid the waiter, then sat back and watched Didi's colour heighten further.

'Shall I tell you what I'm thinking about?' he went on when the waiter had moved away. He leaned closer so he could see flecks of gold amongst the silver in her eyes. 'I'm thinking about peeling those clothes off you. Slowly. Then sampling every inch of your skin. With my hands. With my tongue. Every inch.' He let his gaze travel over the swell of her breasts. 'Or maybe I'll savour the anticipation and let you strip while I watch before I—'

'I'm thinking *you* should get naked first.' The colour had bled into her neck. Her eyes flicked to his lap. 'I want to watch you get turned on.'

Just the thought of those eyes stroking him with liquid heat shot bullets of fire to his groin. 'Too late,' he murmured, watching her eyes widen, her pupils dilate. 'I already am.'

'Well, then.' She picked up her cup, sipped, her expression touched by the humour of it. 'It's too bad we have a twenty-five-minute walk ahead of us. In the cold.'

Suddenly he didn't want to make that long chilly walk. A stroll, for Pete's sake, what had he been thinking? He took a long gulp of whisky to wet his lust-dry throat. 'We can be in a warm room in ten minutes.'

She laughed, a tinkling erotic sound. 'You think so?'

He grinned back. 'I know so.' In ten minutes they could both be naked and warm and feeling really really good. Why waste another moment? He felt the grin drop away from his lips. Didi could make him feel good, and a lot more—she could help him forget. 'What do you say? Are you game?'

She blinked. 'You're serious. Here?'

'You better believe it.' He lifted his glass to his lips to savour the whisky's aroma.

'You mean we're going to rock up at check-in with no luggage and ask for a room and a "by the way, do you charge by the hour?"' She set her cup on its saucer with a clink. 'How many couples check in to five-star luxury for a quick roll over the sheets?'

'Who says it's going to be quick?'

Her eyes turned a smoky grey, an early morning heatwave haze with a voice to match. 'How many hours do you think we might need, Cameron?' It continually fascinated him; her innocence-in-black-lace routine.

'Whatever it takes.' He polished off his whisky in one long draught. 'As long as we're home before six-thirty.'

She checked her watch, slurped a few mouthfuls of tea, picked up her coat and rose. 'Better get started, then.'

'Ah, a small problem.' He glanced down at himself. Maybe not so small...

She leaned in, her small breasts brushing against his forearm as she whispered in his ear. 'Stay close behind and come with me.'

He reached for her cool slim fingers, entwined them with his. 'I intend to do just that, sweetheart.'

'Hurry.' The urgency in Didi's voice sharpened his anticipation to a razor's edge.

'Going as fast as I can,' Cameron muttered, swiping the key-card for the second time, his free hand still locked with hers.

Finally. He tugged her hand and they spilled into the room like a couple of horny teenagers, tossing handbag and jackets on the floor and not bothering with lights. Only the master lamp cast a muted yellow pool in the room's foyer.

'Didi...' He whirled, pressing her against the

door so he could ravish her mouth the way he'd been wanting to since early this morning. His blood pounded into life, roaring through his veins. Already he'd committed her taste to memory, the scent of her skin, the sound of her moan as her mouth opened beneath his.

Their joined hands brushed the front of his jeans; he wasn't sure who'd made the move, didn't care. He took advantage, rubbing her knuckles over his throbbing erection while his tongue dived over hers. This fever of need wasn't anything he'd not experienced before but this strange vicelike grip in the region of his heart was new.

So he'd die of a heart attack in the throes of passion. He'd die a happy man. But he lifted his head, let them both catch their breath. Her breasts rose and fell in rapid succession, hard nipples abrading his chest through their combined layers of worn jersey.

'I want to see if you're as beautiful as I remember,' he muttered, and tugged her T-shirt over her head. Tossed it over his shoulder. Dragged the bra cups down and filled his palms with warm female flesh.

Her skin was rich cream against his darker hands, delicate and fragrant, her nipples pale and tight. Impossible not to taste. He captured one, scraped over it with teeth and tongue. She hauled in a whimpered breath, tracked fingernails through his scalp. Urgency pinched at his flesh. He wanted those fingers on other, more needy parts.

'And…?'

She tugged his head away from her breast with the palms of her hands and he fell into her eyes. 'You're…' *not what I expected* '…enchanting.'

What was happening here? Was this more than sex?

He thrust the questions from his mind. It would *not* be more. Peeling them both away from the door, he lifted her off her feet and quickstepped them to the foot of the bed.

He grabbed his wallet from his jeans as he toppled her onto the mattress and followed her down, hot, impatient, wild for her. His fingers fumbled with the leather a moment, then closed over the foil package. He held it up in front of her face. 'The only condom I have with me.'

Her hand snapped up to cover his, eyes dark with a wicked promise of approaching turbulence. 'Better make the most of it, then.'

* * *

Cameron caught her hand before it slid off his sweat-slick belly. He didn't want to move yet; he was enjoying the feel of her body tucked against his. 'So…you said you've seen it all before.'

'I've always felt an obligation to try and help out where I can. There was a halfway house for those undergoing drug rehab…' She moved her head side to side against his shoulder, her fragrant hair tickling his chin. 'Well, you know how it is.'

He did. And the fact that she did too was a connection he hadn't anticipated. He was still mulling that over when she rolled onto her stomach, tugging the sheet with her, and traced a finger down the centre of his chest.

'But you… You let me believe all you were interested in was money.'

He hesitated. 'For a long time it was. Because growing up I didn't have it.' He should have moved. He should have known she'd ask questions. And he should have thought before he answered. Even in the semi-darkness he felt the incredulity in her eyes.

'What? Money?'

'Surprised, Didi?' His private smile was humourless. 'Seems we've traded places.'

She was silent a moment. 'You know about my family, tell me about yours.'

His lips turned numb, the black hole that had been his life yawned before him. A life that distanced him for ever from Didi's world. He pushed her hand away. 'You don't want to hear about my family.'

'I want to know what motivates a man to build a centre for runaways,' she said quietly. 'To invest not only money but time and interest. I saw how you were with those kids. Why?'

He shrugged, turned away from those perceptive eyes. But Lizzie's collapse tonight had wrung his emotions dry. He expelled a long sigh. 'Because I keep hoping that one day my sister will walk through those doors.'

'You have a sister?'

His body tensed as the old pain around his heart clenched its fist. 'Listen, can we just drop this?'

'No. Tell me about her.'

He'd already discovered Didi's tenacity and since he'd already opened his mouth... 'Amy. I don't know where she is, or even if she's still alive. The last time I saw her I was eighteen and doing what I could to keep us together, she was seventeen and on drugs.'

'Where were your parents?'

'Dead.' His voice sounded flat and devoid of emotion. Experience had taught him emotion made one vulnerable. He didn't intend to be vulnerable, to anything, or anyone ever again.

'Oh, Cameron. I'm sorry.'

That old cliché. 'Don't be.' He clenched his jaw against a rising anger that had nothing—and everything—to do with Didi. What the hell would she know with her childhood of opportunities? 'It's the familiar story of drugs and domestic violence.'

'It might help if you t—'

'Leave it alone, Didi. It's ancient history and nothing to do with you.'

Wanting distance, he rolled out of bed and crossed to the window. He didn't need the woman with her sympathy and sad eyes. Instead he watched the reflections in the river, a late train snaking into Flinders Street Station. For the first time in years he desperately craved a cigarette.

But memories of a childhood he kept ruthlessly buried flashed before him. Wanted fugitive, Bernie Boyd had died during a police chase, Cam's mother of a prescription drug overdose a few months later.

His biggest mistake had been confiding all to Katrina, and hadn't she had her moment of glory with the poster campaign? *He's not the man you think he is.*

He would not make the same mistake with Didi.

'Come back to bed, Cameron.'

Her arms slid around his back, her hands splayed over his chest—not provocative or teasing—just... easy. Soothing. He hadn't heard her approach but she was warm and suddenly very welcome. Her hair felt like soft warm rain against his skin. He knew if he looked into her eyes he'd see understanding. She didn't understand of course, but she cared. Perhaps she wouldn't if she knew, but for now it was enough that she was here.

Wordlessly he turned into her embrace.

Where he knew he was wanted.

Where he wanted to be.

He showed her how much with nips and open-mouth kisses beneath her ear, down her throat, while he let his hands glide over the dips and curves. How good they could be together—*were* together.

She responded with little murmurs and sighs. No words. As if she understood he didn't want them. She seemed to know just what he needed, yet how could she? She'd known him a matter of days.

Warmth stole through him like a thief, catching him unawares. He'd been damn rude to her—how long had it been since any woman had shown him anything approaching compassion? And he'd cut her off.

He wanted to hold her again in a fever of passion and have her body once more, apologise, but the strength had drained out of him. So he stroked her hair and simply held her. Within her aura he could forget the dark and live in the light.

As long as he kept his past private, so long as he didn't let emotion get the upper hand, there was no reason they couldn't continue what they'd started.

Didi woke to the pink pearl light of morning, the conversation they'd had before they'd fallen asleep fresh in her mind. She could still feel Cameron's emotional scars as if they were carved into his flesh, and wanted to weep. And comfort.

But when she opened her eyes and turned to him she discovered she was alone. A note written on the hotel's stationery lay on the crisp white pillow beside her.

Good morning, Didi,
I've gone to the hospital to check on Lizzie
before I head in to the office...

She frowned. He worked on a Saturday? Yeah,
that sounded like him. She read on.

Sleep in for a bit, ring room service and
order up breakfast; it's already paid for. I've
arranged for a taxi to take you home when
you're ready, speak to Concierge. Have a pro-
ductive day. Cam.
PS I'll feed Charlie on my way, no need to
rush.
PPS Thank you for last night.

She basked in the warm glow of his PPS for
a few seconds. Then shook it off. *Silly girl.* He
hadn't meant last night as in *last night*—the way
she wanted him to mean last night—he meant her
help at the community centre.
Didn't he?
He'd booked the cab and paid for breakfast. So
despite his own problems he'd thought of her well-
being this morning. *Don't get used to it.* He was
pampering her because he wanted her *productive.*

So she sat up in bed, dialled room service and ordered the biggest breakfast on the menu, since she'd not indulged in that particular luxury in a long time.

She fluffed her pillows, pulled the sheet up to her chin and lay back to wait for her meal. Theirs wasn't a relationship where they shared intimacies of the family kind; at least on his part. It was all about business—he wanted an artist who could deliver a product.

And it was all about sex. Great sex, the hottest sex she'd ever had. With the most attentive lover she'd ever known. But it was still sex without intimacy.

A problem. Because against all her good intentions to adhere to the rules they'd agreed on she was falling for him—her casual no-strings walk-away-when-it's-done lover. Which should *not* mean she wanted to know him better on a personal level. She should *not* want to know more about his family.

A sixth sense told her there was more to the situation than drugs and violence. How to get him to open up—or not—was the million-dollar question. Would it draw them closer or push them apart?

* * *

'Hi.'

Didi's needle slipped, spilling the gold beads she was threading as her heart did a little flutter. Scooping them into her palm, she put them back in their container and looked at him over her glasses. 'Hi.'

She hadn't heard Cameron come in over the sound of the stereo. He was wearing khaki trousers and a casual navy shirt. He looked a little ragged around the edges. Running on the little amount of sleep he must have had, she wasn't surprised. Her heart fluttered again at the reason for his lack of shut-eye. 'How's Lizzie?'

'She's lucky. She's going to be okay.'

Didi nodded. 'Thanks to you.' She studied him a moment. 'Do you always work on the weekend?'

'When it's necessary.' He stared at her a moment with those blueberry eyes, a bemused smile on his lips. 'For days you've had me wondering... Why the pink lenses?'

'Because then everything looks rosy on the greyest of days. Even you.' Smiling at him, unreasonably happy to see him, she took them off, rubbed the bridge of her nose, then stretched her arms up and out and wiggled her fingers.

She'd worked all day. She had spray glitter on her leggings, needle-stab wounds in her fingers and beads from here to Christmas, but she'd made darn good progress.

He wasn't looking at her progress.

He was watching her nipples prickle and tighten beneath her T-shirt. Her nipples hadn't had such a workout since…never, she decided, and lowered her arms slowly. 'Um…so…what do you think?'

'Very nice.'

'You haven't even looked,' she accused. She knew because she'd had her eyes on his since she'd caught him standing there.

'I've looked.' He crossed the room. 'I've been here at least thirty seconds watching you work.'

'Oh.' He'd seen her naked, there wasn't an inch he hadn't seen, yet still she felt the blush bloom on her cheeks.

'Watching and imagining you wearing nothing but those pink glasses and eating apples. Red apples.'

Her blush deepened and she flapped a hand. 'What is it with you and apples?'

He smiled. 'Just a little fantasy of mine.' Still smiling, he held out a slim box she'd not noticed. 'For a hard day's work.'

'Ah-h-h.' She ripped off the paper, opened the lid. An assortment of exclusive, handmade dark chocolates.

'Soft centres,' he said as he plucked one out and slipped it between her lips. 'I promised you chocolate.'

Its decadent cream flowed over her tongue. 'Mmm.' She beamed at him. 'Thank you.'

'You're supposed to share.'

'Of course. Sorry. Which would you like?'

'You choose.'

She checked the guide, then rose. 'Honey myrtle.' And pressed it against his lips. He opened his mouth, closed his lips over her fingers and for a moment…

'Right now I have this image of you wearing those glasses—just the glasses—while I feed you chocolate.'

'Not apples?'

'No. I'd bite it in half—*sharing*—and drizzle your half of the cream between your lips.'

Her eyes glazed over at the image. 'That could work.'

The intercom buzzed and the phone rang simultaneously. 'That'll be our meal,' Cameron said, withdrawing his wallet and tossing it on the table. 'I ordered Chinese. Can you get it? Money's there.'

As Didi paid off the delivery girl she noticed a creased photo in Cameron's wallet. A young woman.

An instant punch to her solar plexus. 'That was quick,' she said as Cameron disconnected, juggling their meal and squinting at the photo and trying not to look as if she was before she flipped the wallet shut.

'One of those pesky call centres,' he groused. 'Don't they have weekends in India? If you're wondering who it is,' he said, relieving her of the food, 'that's Amy.'

'I wasn't prying.' *Much.* But she moved to the table and picked up her spectacles for a better look. 'I've seen this girl...'

She felt the instant tension as Cameron stiffened beside her. 'Where?' he asked sharply.

She struggled to remember. The shape of the girl's face, the hair colour... She couldn't have seen her—what would be the odds? She closed the wallet, put it on the table. She shouldn't have mentioned it. *Stupid.* 'I'm probably seeing the family resemblance.' She smiled at the tight-lipped man in front of her and teased, 'She looks like you on a good day.'

'She'd be thirty-one now—she'd've changed.'

'Exactly.' She shook away the odd feeling and changed the subject. 'Let's eat. I'm starving.'

Ten minutes later they were tucking into sweet chilli roast pork and king prawn combination.

'I've got a fund-raising dinner next Saturday night,' Cameron said between mouthfuls. 'I want you to accompany me.'

The sudden punch of nerves caught Didi off guard. 'Are you sure?' She'd known it was likely. But being seen in public as his partner, however temporary, was something new. She had no idea what type of woman he usually dated, but she knew she wouldn't fit in. She'd never fitted in with the elite. She'd be more of an embarrassment. 'Perhaps it's better if you just go on your own.'

'Of course I'm sure, and, no, I'm not going on my own—I've already paid for two tickets. The money raised is going towards a dozen local charities. You'll want to come—this'll be a good opportunity to talk about your art, mention the gallery opening and make some contacts.'

The alternative would be to chaperone another woman...

There *was* no alternative.

She bit off a corner of bamboo shoot, then nodded. 'Okay.'

On the inside her stomach was churning. How would his business associates view her? Would they know she was only his short-term lover?

And what the heck was she going to wear?

CHAPTER ELEVEN

'I GUESS my sequined leggings and macramé top are out?' Didi murmured, only half joking. She liked the glitzy outfit she'd bought at a recycle boutique. It made her feel happy and it drew looks whenever she wore it. She also knew her taste didn't conform to the conventional fashion trends.

Cameron looked up, his mouth open in astonishment. 'This is a formal dinner, Didi. The "rich and famous" will be there. You'll need to wear something suitable. A dress.'

She scowled down at her half-eaten meal. 'I don't own a dress.' Not any more.

'I told you I'd pay for whatever you need. Leave it with me. My secretary, Chris, knows how to shop and what's appropriate. Write down your dress size and preferences and I'll have her send around some items for you to choose from.'

His condescending attitude sent prickles up her spine and she stiffened. 'I've attended a few of these formal shindigs in my time,' she said coolly. 'You think I don't know what's appropriate?'

He stared at her and she could see him trying to dig his way out of the hole he'd got himself in. 'Of course you do,' he said placatingly. In that same condescending tone. 'But I know you're busy here. I'm just trying to save you some time.'

He had a point. She couldn't afford to fall any further behind.

In two weeks their working relationship would be over. Their private relationship would be over. A stark reminder that this was a temporary arrangement and she'd be better off remembering that. But a hollow feeling opened up inside her.

'You'll find something we both like,' he went on, oblivious to her inner turmoil. Mr Super Confident twirled his chopsticks through his meal, picked up a prawn.

She needed to retain her independence and some control over her life. Their tastes were light years apart—she'd seen the way he looked at her clothes. But what he liked wouldn't matter in two weeks. 'I still have that cash you gave me. You don't need to fork out any more.'

'That's an advance on your commission. It has

nothing to do with this.' He glanced at her, his smile indulgent. 'Call the dress a gift.'

A gift. Wasn't that what men like him gave their mistresses? Oh, how she hated that word. She hated that that was all he wanted from her. She realised she wanted so much more. A chill wrapped around her heart. *Don't you dare cry.* Instead she dared herself to look him in the eye and ask, 'Would that be for services rendered, then?'

His smile disappeared, his eyes locked on hers. 'Didi.' He put down his chopsticks, stood and rounded the table. Crouched in front of her and took her face between his hands. 'You know damn well that's not what I meant.'

She'd never heard his voice so quiet, so firm. It wrapped around her like blue velvet. No, Didi thought, he wasn't at all sure how she'd interpreted him. Maybe she wasn't so sure herself. And when had he become more to her than a casual lover?

He *couldn't* be more; she couldn't let him.

'Hell...Didi.' He smoothed his thumbs over her cheeks. His eyes glinted in the down-lights. 'If I insulted you, I apologise. I want you with me on Saturday night. Only you.'

Her heart melted and a smile tugged at her lips.

'Ah, but would you want me with you in my sequined leggings and macramé top?'

His eyes flickered, then he blew out a slow breath. 'Can we compromise on this? If Chris organises some stuff for you to look at and you don't like anything...' He rubbed his lips over hers. 'Let's just see how it goes with Chris first. Now...come up here.'

He stood, taking her with him, lifting her higher so that his body bits lined up with hers in all the right places. Their mouths feasted on one another's as he headed for the black rug between the sofas. He laid her down on its luxurious pile, his hands diving beneath her top.

'Do we have a deal?' he murmured against her mouth.

Her own hands got busy with his belt buckle. 'Deal.'

The next few days passed in a blur. During the day Cameron worked at the office. Mostly. And they kept things platonic—well, almost. If you didn't count Monday's lunchtime session in the spa or the interlude in the sky garden. Her exhibition piece was growing, taking shape slowly but surely.

One of Cameron's employees took Charlie. Didi was devastated to see him go, but happy he'd found a safe new home where he'd be cared for. One day perhaps she could have him back. She missed him. *Get used to it*—very soon she'd be missing Cameron as well.

In the evenings they went out for a quick bite or purchased dinner from the numerous takeaway stores nearby. Either way, they walked, taking in the fresh evening air so Didi could stretch her legs after working all day in the one spot. And every night was another magical journey of discovery.

The dresses were delivered to the apartment on Tuesday. A boutique full of beautiful expensive designer outfits. Accessories. Shoes. Any woman would have been beside herself. Didi wasn't any woman.

Did Cameron want to help her decide? she phoned to ask. No. Anything the lovely Chris chose was sure to be a knockout and he was looking forward to seeing Didi all dressed up on Saturday night. And by the way—had he told her?—Chris had booked her in to Tiara's Spa and Beauty—*the* latest 'in' place—for Saturday afternoon. The massage and hot stone treatment would do her good.

It wasn't the massage she worried about. No hairdresser had come within cutting distance of her hair in a long time. She trimmed it herself with the aid of mirrors. And make-up? She didn't bother with more than the basics of foundation, lip gloss and blusher.

Compromise. They'd made some compromises over the past week and Didi was realising it didn't mean she had to give up her control or her independence. That she could look at a situation from another's point of view, another's needs. But this transformation? She wasn't so sure.

A stranger stared back at Didi in her mirror on Saturday evening. A sophisticated-looking woman in a short black organza dress with kohl-rimmed eyes, siren-red glossed lips and her hair carefully styled to wisp softly around her face. At least they hadn't cut it. She wanted to cry, but the truck-load of mascara they'd applied would probably run.

She wanted to run.

She'd seen something she wished she hadn't while flicking through an out-dated magazine at the salon—a photo of Cameron and a stunning brunette almost as tall as he was. The don't-date-him poster girl? Possibly. The woman on the other end of the mystery phone calls? Again, possibly. How could she compete with that kind of woman?

She could hear Cameron pacing the marble floor beyond. She'd cloistered herself back in her own room since she'd arrived back from her salon appointment. She was now fifteen minutes behind their agreed time.

What would he think when he saw her? Would she come up to scratch? With no hope of competing with women like that brunette, Didi felt the same insecurities that had haunted her when she'd attended functions with her family.

Turning away from the unnervingly false image, she picked up the tiny red velvet evening purse. She wasn't sophisticated, why was she pretending to be someone she wasn't?

Because she was Cameron's partner for the evening. Tonight she'd try to be the poised cosmopolitan woman he expected. She could play the part for one night. One more week, one gallery opening and their no-strings arrangement would be over.

Cameron knocked on her door. 'Ready?'

Her heart gallumphed. Her hands turned clammy and cold. She primed her lips for a smile, took a steadying breath and said, 'Ready as I'll ever be.'

She got a glimpse of dark eyes and clean-shaven jaw as she opened the door. A whiff of aftershave as she ducked under the arm he'd leaned against the jamb and hurried to the hat stand to grab her new black coat, which was part of the package.

'Hey, what's the rush?'

'We're running late, my fault. Sorry.' Her fingers closed over the soft wool but Cameron took it from her.

'We can run a little late,' he said, his deep voice vibrating along her spine, his breath disturbing the hairs on her nape. 'Turn around and let's get a look.'

She almost forgot her own insecurities when she swivelled on her stilettos and got a look at Cameron in full formal get-up. Oh, my… Damn, he looked good. She almost reached out to finger the bow tie and give herself an excuse to drift her knuckles against his throat, until she saw him staring at her as if he'd never seen her before… and remembered why.

She'd gone for elegant black. As she turned Cam stepped back to take in the full effect. The dress hugged her petite figure like a charm. Tiny straps showed off her creamy shoulders, the waistline was cinched with a sparkly clasp. Its short skirt flared, leaving plenty of thigh to admire. And the arch of her feet in those gold strappy heels made his mouth water. 'You look sensational, Didi.'

She smiled, drawing his attention to her carefully outlined lips and the shimmering charcoal framing her silver eyes. He doubted he'd ever escorted a more beautiful woman, but something about the stunning image niggled at him.

She seemed to pick up on that vibe and the smile disappeared. 'Let's go, then,' she said briskly, reaching for her coat draped over his arm.

'Hang on.' He returned her coat to the stand, fingered the box in his pocket. He'd wanted to give her some token, something to show how he felt about her. Even if he wasn't sure yet what that feeling was. Would she be offended? Only one way to find out. He withdrew the box.

She looked at it, then up at him with wary eyes. 'Soft centres…?'

Her voice was unsteady, the way his knees suddenly felt. 'It's just a little something to wear tonight,' he said, holding it out to her. 'I'm not sure if you're a jewellery girl but figured what the heck, a bit of bling couldn't hurt.'

When she made no move to take the box, he opened it himself. The single teardrop gem winked on its glittering chain.

'Is that real?' she whispered, and squinted closer. 'It looks real.'

'It's an Argyle pink diamond on a platinum chain. You being the creative sort, I thought something simple was probably wise.'

She looked up, met his eyes. 'I don't call that simple or wise.'

And didn't that just about sum up their relationship? 'Wear it for me, Didi.' Without waiting for a reply he stepped behind her to slip it around her neck, unaccountably disappointed that her almond-honey scent had been drowned out by cosmetics and styling lotion and a darker cloying fragrance that on any other woman would have been seductive.

On Didi it was just…wrong. She didn't need heavy fragrance to seduce, all she needed to be was herself. Shaking away the dangerous thought, he stepped in front of her again to see how the stone looked against her skin.

She touched the stone lightly with one finger, but her eyes gave him no clue to her feelings, as if she'd deliberately blanked her expression. 'Thank you. It's the most beautiful piece of jewellery I've ever worn.'

'You're welcome.' He wanted to lay his lips on hers and feel them smile against his as she had last night but the slick red gloss looked more like a shield than an invitation. Instead, he reached for her coat. 'Shall we go?'

The hotel ballroom was all glitz. Crystal and silverware sparkled on snowy cloths sprinkled with colourful foil confetti. Towering floral arrangements spilled their early spring fragrance, mingling with French perfume and hors d'oeuvres being circulated on silver trays.

Cam lifted two glasses of champagne as a waiter passed. Then he saw a tall slim blonde wearing gold leopard-skin lamé as if she'd been born in it heading in their direction.

'Let's find out where we're seated,' he murmured to Didi, handing her a glass and turning away.

'Cam.' The woman caught at his arm. 'You weren't trying to run away, were you, darling? I know you'll want to buy a ticket or three in tonight's raffle.' She swept between him and Didi waving her little box of tickets, then reached up to buss both his cheeks.

He forced a smile. Dominique was in her mid-forties and had been pursuing him for at least five years. 'Evening, Dominique.' He stepped around her to create a triangle. 'I'd like you to meet Didi O'Flanagan. Didi, this is Dominique Le Hunte. She's our fund-raiser extraordinaire.'

'Di-di.' Dominique's latest Botox treatment prevented her eyebrows rising but she tinkled out a laugh. 'What a quaint little abbreviation.' She proffered a limp hand dripping with diamonds. 'Why...what's so terrible about your birth name?'

'It's Dee-aahn,' Didi replied with exaggerated aplomb. 'My sister never could get it right so she said Didi. I'm afraid it stuck.'

Cam smiled privately at the way Didi's lie rolled off her tongue and raised his glass to her with an intimate grin that had Dominique frowning. Or would if she could, he mused.

'Well—*Dee-aahn*—it's...nice of you to...attend.'

'Certainly is. Very nice,' Didi drawled as she gave Cam a smouldering look and took a long slow sip of champagne.

Dominique didn't have a comeback.

Cam cleared his throat to cover a chuckle and signalled a waiter bearing spring rolls. Not many people stopped Dominique in her tracks. But then hadn't Didi O'Flanagan stopped Cam himself in his tracks?

Dominique recovered enough to turn on the charm again. 'So where did you two meet?'

Cam smiled at Didi, remembering the event-filled evening with a certain fondness and said, 'At a function a few weeks back.'

'I was waitressing, actually,' Didi said with dead calm, meeting his eyes as she plucked a roll off the proffered plate. 'Thank you.' This directed at the waiter with a sunny smile.

'Oh…' Dominique laughed uncertainly and glanced at Cam. 'Helping out in a volunteer capacity?'

'Making a living.' Didi bit into her spring roll.

'Making a living?' Dominique echoed faintly.

'I've commissioned Didi to complete an arts project for me,' Cam cut in to curtail what looked like developing into a 'situation'. He placed his hand on her back, cruised it up the black fabric till he found skin. Heaven knew what Didi was capable of under such circumstances. He nudged her forward, excusing them both. 'I think they're about to start seating us and we haven't found our table yet. Catch you later, Dominique.'

'Rich bitch,' Didi muttered beneath her breath. 'Your friends—'

'They're not my friends. They're mostly business associates. It's important to project the correct image at these events.'

He felt her spine stiffen beneath his hand. 'Yeah, and haven't I heard *that* before.'

'I—'

'Do you have friends, Cameron?' She stopped mid-stride to look up at him. 'And I don't mean bed partners.'

A muscle in his jaw ticced. 'Yes, of course I do. That's our table.' He prompted her forward.

But how many could he name? He realised he'd been too busy making his mark in his new life without any links to his past to form any lasting friendships.

Mouth-watering food was served on elegant dishes, the wine flowed, the speeches were made. Didi sat opposite him conversing easily with the people around her, as if she'd been born to it. Which, he had to constantly remind himself, she had.

But every time he looked at her it was like look-

ing at someone else. And when their eyes met—
there it was again—that vulnerable, sad look in
her eyes as her smile dropped away. Just a glimpse
before she snapped her gaze to Lady Johnson beside her and *with a smile* renewed their conversation.

He fingered the stem of his wine glass and
watched her. She was easily the most beautiful
woman in the room, but she wasn't his Didi.

His Didi.

It steamrolled over him with a force that made
his heart thud harder and his muscles cramp and
his hand tighten on his glass till he thought it
might snap. They had one more week. He didn't
want their relationship to end yet. She was like
stepping into spring sunshine after a long cold
winter. He wanted to bathe in that warmth a little
longer. What would she say if he suggested rene-
gotiating their arrangement, extending it a little?

He didn't get a moment to ponder that further
because it was time for the lucky door prize. 'And
the winner is…Didi O'Flanagan,' the MC announced. 'Dinner for two at the Candle-side restaurant. Come on up, Didi O'Flanagan.'

Cam watched her lay her napkin on the table and
make her way to the stage, her short skirt flaring

around her upper thighs. Those silky thighs had rubbed along his only twenty-four hours ago. And again he felt that overwhelming sense of ownership and pride.

And imminent sense of loss.

'And no second guesses, ladies and gentleman, as to the lucky guy sharing the evening with our lovely winner.'

She took possession of the tickets, held them high, then grinned at Cam. The necklace he'd given her winked in the lights. He could only nod, his throat constricted, his chest tight. Couldn't manage a smile. The noise seemed to dim, the crowd faded to black and all he could see was Didi.

But she wasn't Didi. She was dressed and styled like a woman he might have dated a few weeks ago if he hadn't met her. He didn't like the changes; he wanted the old Didi back. The girl with the offbeat fashion sense and spiked hair.

As she watched him her hand fell to her side, her smile faded. He saw her step off the stage and walk back to the table, chin high. But she didn't sit down—she swiped her purse from the table and headed to the Ladies without looking at him.

Cam excused himself from the table and caught

up with her as she exited a few moments later. She stopped short when she saw him.

The sheen of moisture in her eyes damn near killed him. 'What's wrong?'

She shook her head. 'Nothing.'

So she wasn't going to talk. 'I've had enough,' he said. 'How about you? You want to skip dessert?'

She gave a half-nod. 'But you've spent so much money…'

'I don't give a flying fig about the money.' He took her hand, rubbed his thumb over her knuckles. 'We can splurge on that ice cream in the freezer if you want. We'll grab your coat and escape before anyone else sees us.'

'Cameron… Is that what this is all about?' she asked in a small voice.

He frowned and kept walking, tugging her along beside him. 'Is *what* what this is all about?'

'You don't want anyone to see us together?'

'No, I don't.' He squeezed her hand. 'I just want to go home.'

CHAPTER TWELVE

DIDI hugged her arms as they rode home. Even in her new wool coat she felt cold. Cameron had openly admitted he didn't want to be seen with her. She might look the part tonight but he knew it wasn't the real deal. Unlike that glamorous woman she'd seen on his arm in the magazine.

How could she hope to measure up to that poise and sophistication? Once again she didn't fit. She'd never fit in with the rich crowd. Up on that stage she'd been linked with him publicly and all he'd done was frown.

She'd fallen in love with a man who didn't love her.

Yes, she was in love, time to admit it. When was she going to learn? When was she going to stop letting her heart be broken?

'Would you like that ice cream?' he asked as they entered the apartment. 'Or coffee?'

She kept walking, her stilettos clacking over the marble. 'No, thanks. I'm going to bed.'

All she wanted to do was scrub the gunk off her face, strip out of the dress and hide under the quilt. Alone. But time was running out. Very soon she *would* be alone. Permanently. Because she'd never let this happen again. She closed the en-suite door, kicked off her shoes and reached for her make-up remover.

When she opened the door ten minutes later Cameron was sitting on the edge of the turned-down bed, his shirt unbuttoned, his feet bare. Waiting for her. Yes, he wanted her in the bedroom, just not in public.

His gaze tracked her progress, but it wasn't the look of a man who only wanted sex. For a moment he looked as if he really cared in a deeper, more intimate way.

And it hurt. Because now it seemed she was only seeing what she wanted to see. She'd lost the ability to be objective. And damn it all, she was going to give him what he wanted, because she wanted it too. For the next few nights she'd take what they could make together and store the memories in her heart.

'Didi.' He rose and came to her, touched her cheek with such tenderness she wanted to weep. She let him unzip her dress, tug the straps over her shoulders. It fell to the floor with a soft flutter of air. The blunt tips of his fingers fumbled at her back as he unclasped her bra, drew it away. Then her black lace panties as his palms slipped beneath the elastic and tugged. Over her hips, down her thighs.

Fast or slow, he made love-making an art. With one flick of his finger, one brush of his lips, he knew how to tease and arouse, how to soothe and seduce.

'This is how I want you,' he murmured, tracing a damp path down her body from neck to navel with light nips, fleeting open-mouthed kisses. 'No cosmetics to conceal your inner glow, nothing to hide your naked beauty. Just Didi.'

He knelt before her, his eyes following the path his mouth had taken while his palms massaged slow circles over her hips. The diamond he'd given her burned into the flesh above her breasts as if he'd set it alight with his gaze and she knew then that she'd never take it off.

The lump in her throat made it impossible to speak. She needed to remember his words were just that—words. To pretend they didn't flow into her heart, filling it until it felt ready to burst.

To *not* let her imagination leap ahead to happy-ever-afters as he lifted her against his hard warm body and laid her back on the fine cotton sheets.

To *not* notice how his heart thudded against hers as if they beat as one when he stretched out beside her.

His hands were big, his fingers roughened, but he handled her as if she were made of the most fragile glass. Somehow his trousers were gone, his satin-steel erection sliding hotly against the soft flesh of her belly as he eased on top of her.

His mouth covered hers. He drank her in and reason ebbed away, longing flowed in. He tasted of rich dark wine and spice and summer. But summer was impossibly far away and out of reach so she reached instead for the arms that held her, curled her hands around his rock-hard strength and thought only of the moment.

He slipped like silk inside her. Longing turned to need, and need to urgency. Yet even in passion he paid homage to her with a reverence she'd never experienced.

When he sent her soaring she touched the stars, and he was right there with her. It was a long slow slide back to sanity.

To reality.

To the man who couldn't wait to take her home

because he hadn't wanted to be seen with her. Once again her not-so-smart mouth had got her into trouble. Dominique had pushed all the wrong buttons and Didi had just had to react, hadn't she?

She just bet that woman on his arm in the picture would know how to work a room, what to say, how to say it. Feeling vulnerable, she pulled the sheet higher to cover her breasts. 'I saw your picture in a magazine at the salon today.'

'I hope it was my good side,' Cameron murmured against her temple while his fingernails traced lazy circles on Didi's upper arm.

'You were with a woman.' *Tall, dark. Stunning.* 'Was it Kathryn…?' She felt a quiver of tension run through him.

'Katrina.' He spoke through stiff lips.

'Ah, of course. *Katrina.* Perhaps you should've taken *her* to dinner.'

Tension tightened his hand and he pulled it away from her arm. 'Don't do this, Didi. It was over with her a while ago.'

'Is she the woman who left the poster?'

A long, telling silence. 'She's out of my life.'

From the photos she'd seen of the two of them the woman was not unlike his sister in looks, Didi thought. Did he even realise that? 'Ah, but are you over her?'

'What do you think?' Irritation roughened his voice as he stared at the ceiling.

A politician's answer—not an answer. Her heart—she had to hold the cracked pieces together. Jay hadn't been honest about his previous partner. A month into his relationship with Didi— they'd even picked out the engagement ring and booked the church...

'What if she changed her mind, Cameron? What if she wanted you back, what if her poster game was a ploy for your attention?'

'No. Why would she do that?'

'Because she's not over you?'

'That's b—'

'The phone rang today,' Didi went on. 'And whoever it was hung up when I answered. It's not the first time. Call it woman's intuition but I know it's a woman.'

Another silence. 'She's over me.'

'Perhaps not, if she thought you'd met someone. Maybe she wants you back because she can't bear the thought of you with someone else.'

'You're wrong. For a start she—' Cameron bit back the words that sprang to his tongue. That

Kat, whose father had the top job of Prime Minister firmly in his sights, would have nothing to do with a man whose father had been a criminal wanted over two states.

The sins of the father... His hands tightened into fists, his blood ran like a chill wind through his veins. Beyond the grave and still screwing with his life.

He couldn't tell Didi. He'd confided in Kat and look where that had landed him. The risk of losing this woman who brought the freshness, warmth and promise of spring into his life was too great a risk. He wanted her with him a little longer—was that selfish?

'She what, Cameron?'

'She's getting married.'

He turned his head on the pillow to impress that fact upon her. To look at her...while she stared at the ceiling. Which allowed him a smile when she might not have appreciated it. 'What about your ex?' he said quietly. 'What happened with him?'

She continued to gaze upward for a long silent moment. He thought she wasn't going to answer him but then she said, 'He was good-looking, wealthy, educated at the right schools—a real ladies' man. I didn't know it at the time but he was on the rebound. Then his ex changed her mind… and they lived happily ever after. End of story.'

'I'm sorry, Didi.'

'Don't be.' She turned her face to him, eyes wide in the dimness. 'I'm over him. I don't do serious any more.' She resumed her study of the ceiling.

Moonlight etched her profile in silver, the pert nose and kissable lips, the curve of her breasts outlined against the sheet. Like fairy folk she was made for moonlight. Or maybe moonlight had been made for her.

Then a wispy cloud drifted past, a gauze curtain dulling the image and taking his smile with it. Like the way their relationship was headed. He wanted to hold that curtain back for one more moment…another day, another week. A year. Ten years.

How long would this infatuation last?

If that was what it was. It felt more like… No. He refused to acknowledge anything deeper. As she'd said, she didn't do serious, neither did he. But how long would it be before Didi wanted more than an affair? A man with his past, his inability to lay his heart on the line and trust, couldn't give her that.

Whatever they had, it would all end in a matter

of days. And that would be the wiser course, he thought. But he couldn't stop himself reaching out to brush her hair off her brow, to gently close her eyelids with his fingers. 'I was the luckiest man there tonight,' he whispered. 'You were gorgeous.'

Her eyelids fluttered against his hand and she turned to him, eyes wide. 'But you couldn't wait to get me away.'

'Only because I wanted you all to myself.'

'You mean you weren't embarrassed?'

'Embarrassed?' He took a moment to figure it out. Was *that* what it was all about? He reached for her hand on the sheet between them, brought it to his cheek. 'Ah, sweetheart...no. *No.* Not on your life. I was *sorry.* I pushed you into something that made you uncomfortable. I tried to make you into someone you're not—with the best of intentions—and that was my mistake.'

She blinked. 'Thank you. For telling me.'

But she knew he hadn't answered all her questions and he hated the deception. It was there in her quiet gaze and the emotional distance she'd put between them.

Didi didn't have time or the emotional energy to think about Cameron and their relationship for the next few days. Instead she poured everything into her work. The piece was coming together beautifully, just as she'd imagined when she'd planned it.

She knew Cameron was busy with preparations for Saturday night's opening, which was perhaps why she saw very little of him, until he slipped into bed beside her at night.

They made love. Sometimes he was warm and tender, at other times it was with an urgency that blew her away; almost as if he didn't want what they had to end. But he never mentioned it, so neither did she. After all, they'd agreed she would walk away at the end, no strings, so she had to assume that hadn't changed. Perhaps if she didn't have the opening coming up she'd have left earlier because it was tearing her apart inside.

He took her to the gallery one evening and showed her the renovations he'd made to the old building. Her Before the Temptation was to be on display, earlier pieces were going to be offered for sale with work from other unknown artists he wanted to support. And then there was the wall where her commissioned piece would hang.

Excitement mingled with a sense of surrealism. Could this really be happening? He'd invited Melbourne's rich and important people. To see *her* work. To launch *her* career. The press coverage was going to be huge.

She'd sent her own invitation to her parents and one to Veronica and Daniel, but had already received an inability to attend from Veronica by return mail. Would her parents treat her with the same indifference?

On Wednesday morning she needed more beads. She stepped out of the building onto the busy footpath and into sunshine where spring was putting in an early appearance. Two trams rattled past, ferrying commuters. Didi rolled stiff shoulders and began walking.

Until she caught sight of the girl she'd seen before near the apartment building. Hard to mistake the six-foot brunette and she was wearing the same velvet jacket she had worn before. And as on those previous occasions, her face was averted and she was hurrying away, disappearing into the swirl of pedestrians.

Didi pivoted on her heel and followed the woman for a few minutes, caught up with her as she was turning into a shopping mall. Her pulse kept time with her fast pace. She had to be right, had to... Didi's hand grasped velvet. The woman jerked, turned. Startled blue eyes met Didi's and she knew she'd been right. 'You're Amy.'

Her eyes darted behind Didi.

'It's okay. I'm Didi and I'm alone. He doesn't know.'

Amy stared at her. 'How do *you* know?'

'He carries your photo in his wallet.' Didi nodded. 'I've seen you near the apartment. I'm surprised he hasn't seen you too.'

'It's been close a couple of times.' Amy twisted her hands around her bag strap. 'He's still got my photo?'

'He wants you in his life, Amy.' When she just stood there, Didi continued. 'You've rung the apartment.'

Amy nodded as tears filled her eyes. 'Then I just chicken out. And he's nearly caught me outside the building...more than once. I turn away, then wish I hadn't.'

Didi slid her arm through Amy's. 'Let's find somewhere to talk...'

'Cameron puts a message in the missing persons column in the paper every month. That's how I know his phone number,' Amy said, stirring her coffee.

'So why haven't you contacted him?'

She stared at her cup. 'He'll think I'm after his money. I was a drug addict... Did he tell you?'

Didi scooped the froth off her cappuccino and watched her. 'Yes.'

'I've cleaned up my life. I've even got a job—only a sales assistant—but I'd like to study some day. I'm saving up.'

'Doesn't the fact he's put an ad in the missing persons tell you anything? He doesn't care about your past. He'd help you. He's set up a centre for kids and there's a new gallery opening this weekend. And you know why? Because he thinks about you. All the time. Let me help.' Didi reached out and covered Amy's hand. 'I'll arrange for you to meet; somewhere neutral if you like. Give me your phone number.' Didi pulled out her mobile.

'You won't tell him? Until I'm ready?'

'No. He doesn't even have to know it's you he'll be meeting. Let's make it Sunday.'

'Sunday?' Amy paled, her hand tightening on her cup. 'That's too soon.'

'No. It's not. He's been looking for you for too many years. I need your word, and I need your phone number.'

Amy nodded. 'Okay. Might as well get it over.'

She gave Didi her number, Didi stored it in her phone, then slipped it back in her bag. 'Remember, he loves you. Now, let's you and I get to know each other.'

'Calm down, you look fantastic and everything's under control,' Cameron reassured her as they headed into the gallery.

It was early, no one was here yet, but in half an hour the place would be full. Full of people who would be looking at her work. Influential people. Judging her creativity. Analysing her style and probably comparing it with Sheila's.

Bats were flapping their wings in her stomach; she'd kill for a glass of water. Or something stronger. She wiped her palms down her thighs as they entered the gallery. 'Oh...'

On the feature wall. *The Eternal Flame. Artist: Didi O'Flanagan.*

She couldn't help it; she rushed over and traced her name with a finger, tears springing to her eyes. 'I can't believe it.'

'Believe it,' said the deep voice she'd become so familiar with.

She took a few steps backwards for the full effect and looked at it through someone else's eyes.

Vermilion silk threads leapt from the background of black silk. Living flames insinuating themselves in an abstract yet intricate design around silver filigree and smoked driftwood.

A glance around showed her smaller pieces amongst other artists' works. Her Temptation piece hung by itself on another wall.

'You'll be taking a lot of orders tonight, I guarantee it. Congratulations.'

'You've done a wonderful job with the displays. Thank you. For everything.' Their eyes met. This was it. Soon it would be time to say goodbye. Her commission was finished, their time was up. Why did the happiest night of her life have to be the saddest?

Cam saw the emotion in her eyes but, hard as it was to keep from responding, he wasn't saying anything yet. Later tonight he hoped to talk her into staying on longer. Perhaps, just perhaps, he could even think about taking their relationship to a new level. Although what that new level might look like was still unclear.

She looked stunning, as unique as her art. Like a model in a fashion magazine. Leggings in fabric of a black and white geometric puzzle reached to mid calf. She wore a sleeveless T-shirt in a similar pattern topped with a macraméd concoction of thin strips of grey leather and burgundy wooden beads. A heavy necklace of similar beads in dark red, black and ivory hung to her waist. Five wooden beaded bracelets adorned her arms. She had silver glitter in her spiked hair.

And he knew she wore his diamond necklace hidden next to her skin.

Two hours later he watched her talking animatedly with an art critic while photographers snapped pictures. She'd spoken to a throng of journalists. He'd heard her being touted as an emerging star in the art world. People were buying; not only her works but others. Champagne flowed as artists he'd supported celebrated.

'She's talented,' a female voice said behind him to another woman beside her.

Pride swelled inside him. Of course she was.

'Yes,' the other woman replied. 'She dropped off the social scene a few years ago. There were rumours…I heard she was virtually stood up at the altar.'

Cam stiffened, tempted to turn around and demand to know it all.

'Really?' The woman's interest was clearly piqued by this information.

'Such a shame; she was so looking forward to setting up house and starting a family. She was devastated. You know who she is, don't you? James O'Flanagan's daughter.'

James O'Flanagan? Didi's father—her family—was up there with royalty amongst Sydney's elite?

Shock slammed Cam mid-chest. His entire body felt as if it were losing structure, his foundations collapsing around him. How could he not have realised? He should have connected the name.

And it changed everything.

Bernie Boyd's son and James O'Flanagan's daughter…impossible. His hands balled into fists in his pockets. The press would waste no time digging up the dirt on him, tabloids would have a field day, and Didi's reputation as an emerging artist would be ruined—the public were an unforgiving lot.

Not to mention what James himself would have to say.

Cam didn't know the man personally but the way he'd treated his daughter was beneath contempt. At least Veronica had sent her apologies; she had a prior engagement, which apparently took precedence over her sister's special night. Her parents hadn't even acknowledged her invitation and Cam knew she was disappointed. What did that say about them?

He shuddered to think what the news about his background would do to the new career she'd fought so hard for. Here was Cam about to suggest their relationship continue. Unthinkable now. As if James O'Flanagan would approve of a live-in relationship for his daughter with the son of a criminal—hell, did O'Flanagan already know?

And Cam couldn't offer her anything more. Didi might not judge him the way Katrina had but she hadn't been totally honest about who she was either—what else hadn't she told him?

She hadn't told him she wanted a home and family some day.

And she deserved it—but he couldn't give her that, not with his background and his inability to commit. Better to get tonight over with as soon as and as sensitively as possible.

Feeling as if she were dancing on clouds, Didi floated out of the elevator then twirled around and planted a kiss on Cameron's mouth. 'Wasn't it wonderful? Spectacular? I'm a success! They're publishing an article in *Textiles* magazine *and The*

Age. A TV interview, three more commissions—*huge* commissions—and every piece sold!'

Cameron smiled against her lips. 'I never doubted it. *You* were wonderful.' He kissed her again, his arms tightening around her. 'Spectacular.'

She wanted to linger a moment more but it seemed Cameron had other ideas because he broke contact and stepped back. 'Why the mysterious expression?' she asked.

'I have a surprise.'

'Am I going to like it? You look kind of...' Sad. Troubled. Now that she thought about it, he'd been quiet most of the way home. Probably because he hadn't been able to get a word in.

As he opened the apartment door the scent of flowers drifted out. She stared in disbelief. Bowls of roses covered every available surface. 'Oh... You arranged all this?' Her heart slammed against her chest as she took in the dining room. The finest dinnerware gleamed, two candles flickered in the centre of the table, their glow reflected in the night-darkened window. A bottle of champagne cooled in an ice-bucket. Dreamy Frank Sinatra love songs wafted from the stereo.

Romance, she thought. Who knew that Cameron Black knew how to do romance? Anticipation flickered along her veins like fireflies as he pulled out a chair.

'Sit,' he told her as he took a crisp napkin from her plate. He set it on her lap, then uncovered the silver dishes. 'I knew you wouldn't have time to eat at the gallery.'

'You were right,' she said, eyeing the supper. A plate of cold Italian antipasto, smoked salmon and capers with lemon wedges. A green salad. Two fluted glasses filled with a rainbow of exotic fruits, jelly and cream.

Again her stomach was jittering, her heart racing. A man didn't go to all this trouble unless he had something important to say. Did he?

He popped the cork, poured the bubbly and handed her a glass before sitting down himself and raising his own. 'To your success, Didi.'

His eyes, she thought, such emotion in his eyes. Anticipation fizzed inside her like the champagne bubbles tickling her nose. 'To *our* success. Your gallery—the whole complex—is going to help so many people.'

With their gazes spearing each other across the table they took a sip, set their glasses down. She waited, breathless for him to say something more.

He forked some antipasto onto her plate, then his own. 'What are your plans now, Didi?'

She blinked. *Her* plans? That wasn't what she'd expected to hear and the bubbles in her system deflated a little. A lot. She'd hoped he'd suggest some plans that included both of them. Together. 'I...um...I'm not sure yet. It kind of depends...' She waited for him to take her cue.

He bit into a cherry tomato, chewed a long time. 'Stay on here a few more days if you want to think about it. Unwind before you find somewhere else.'

Her heart stopped. Literally stopped. She was surprised it started again because it felt as if he'd sliced it open and her blood seemed to have drained into her feet. How could he sound so... detached after what they'd shared over the past three weeks?

What had she expected? It was over. *When the time's up I walk away, no complications on either side.* The deal—she'd said it herself. And meant it. How could she argue now?

'Thank you. But I'll be looking for somewhere tomorrow.' Her voice seemed to be coming from outside her. On the stereo Old Blue Eyes was singing about only having eyes for you, dear. Cameron couldn't have made a worse choice in music if he'd tried.

His eyes didn't meet hers as he said, 'There's no rush.'

'Oh, I think there is.'

He reached out, touched her fingers. 'It's been fun, hasn't it?'

'Fun.' She remembered their first kiss. *It was fun, Cameron.* Her own words mocked her.

'I've enjoyed our time together.'

'Yes...' She pulled her fingers away. He let her.

'Didi. The trick is not taking these kinds of arrangements too seriously.'

'You're so right. If you'll excuse me, I feel a migraine coming on. I... Thank you for...' she waved a trembling hand over the table '...this.' Somehow she made herself stand. 'If you don't mind, I'll need to sleep it off on my own. I'll just grab my stuff...'

Clutching her toiletries and fisting hot tears away, she closed the spare bedroom door behind her, leaned back against it. What had that poster said? *He's not the man you think he is.* She still didn't know what Katrina had meant by that, but she'd been right: he wasn't.

He was more.
And somehow that was worse.
It was over.

CHAPTER THIRTEEN

CAM braced his arms on the table, mashed his lips together and forced himself not to react visibly in any way as he watched Didi disappear down the passage. But inside…

Inside, some black beast was using Cam's heart as a punching bag. He had to clamp his hands to the table top to stop himself from going after her and telling her what this evening's supper had *really* been about.

Forget the rules they'd made, he'd been going to say. To hell with the three-week agreement. He wanted more, a lot more, and he knew she did too.

Okay, so he didn't do long-term—there'd be no harm in exploring where their relationship might go, right?

Until he'd learned who she was.

Pushing up, he extinguished the candles, killed the music, then scraped the barely touched supper into the bin. He figured neither of them would feel like eating any leftovers from the evening.

He sloshed more champagne into his glass, then took it out to the sky garden to watch the stars. Her big night ruined by this stupid idea of supper. A mistake of gigantic proportions. It could have been a night to celebrate success if their three-week arrangement on the side hadn't happened.

If falling in love with her hadn't happened.

He shook his head, blew out a long breath. For a man who didn't do commitment that was one hell of an admission.

His heart cramped with pain. And guilt. Because his loving her would be the worst thing that could happen to her, and it was all his fault. A man with his background wasn't good enough for Katrina, daughter of a future prime minister. He'd never come up to scratch for someone like James O'Flanagan's daughter.

She must never know.

He hurled his glass against the wall, watched it shatter. Like the pieces of his heart. The heart he'd sworn to keep intact.

He rolled out of bed at five a.m. How could he rest with the knowledge that she was leaving? How could he sleep with her scent on the pillow? Shaking his head to clear the memory of that fra-

grance against her skin, he saw yesterday's discarded clothes still on the floor—typical Didi. He
was about to scoop them up and put them in the
clothes hamper...but that wasn't going to work
any more. She'd have no use for the hamper now.

It would be best all round if he stayed away
today, he thought as he cleared away reminders
of last night in the kitchen. He was still holding
the candlesticks and wondering what he could do
about the roses when Didi put in her appearance.

'Morning.' Her voice betrayed little of the emotion he'd seen last night. Tight, polite. Civilised.
As if they were strangers.

And she had to work bloody hard at it, he
thought. Her lips were a thin slash in a white face,
her eyes shaded by her pink-tinted glasses.

*Because everything looks rosy on the greyest
of days. Even you.*

'Good morning.' His own voice, tight and formal. He set the candlesticks on the kitchen bench
with exaggerated control.

He must remember: *James O'Flanagan's daughter. She needs a career boost, she doesn't need
you.*

She took juice from the fridge, poured herself
a glass. 'I'm packing my stuff. Is it okay to store

what I don't need here until I can make other arrangements?'

'Fine.'

'And my Temptation piece, you will make sure it comes back safely, won't you.'

Ah-h-h… 'Didi… Temptation was sold last night.'

She spun around, her eyes flashing fire. 'It was *not* for sale.'

'I'm sorry. The gallery assistant didn't know. It fetched a tidy sum of money.' And named a five-figure sum.

'Money had nothing to do with it.' But her voice calmed some and he could see her working the figure through and coming up with *Wow*. Still, she said, 'You had *no* right. *No right at all,* to let that happen.'

'The gallery's profits from the sale will go towards a good cause.' He turned away, busied himself wiping down the kitchen sink while he let her think about that. 'I'll be out of your way most of the day so you can take your time.'

'You will be home this evening, won't you?'

He turned back to see her eyes dart to his then away. Wary or concerned? Or something else…

'I can be,' he said, cautious. 'Why?'

She lifted a shoulder, taking an interest in the bottom of her glass. 'It's just I've got that free candlelight dinner. We may as well use it before I go. The table's booked for seven p.m. I'll be busy till then so I'll meet you there.'

Part of him wanted to leap at a second chance, another part warned him that leaping into anything remotely connected with Didi was very unwise at this juncture. He stayed where he was. 'I'd like that.' It was too easy to step closer, to breathe her in. 'We don't have to be strangers.' Friends. Only friends.

She rinsed her glass, busied herself drying it. 'Give me a call when you're in town, then.'

'In town?'

'I'm going home. To Sydney.'

It shouldn't hurt. He shouldn't feel as if he'd been sliced and diced. She was cutting ties, not flesh. An hour's flight away.

A world away.

'Didi, your art, the gallery...' *Me.*

She put the glass away, folded the tea towel precisely and hung it on the rail. 'The beauty of what I do is I can work anywhere. I'll continue to display my work in your gallery, if you want it.'

'Of course I do.'

She turned around, her back against the sink, hands spread either side along the counter top—the counter top where they'd shared that first sky-scraper-demolishing kiss. Her eyes met Cam's and they were clear and direct for the first time this morning. 'It's time to talk with my parents. We have issues to resolve...I'll be staying with them a while.'

'You didn't tell me who your father is.' He could hear the accusation behind his own casually spoken words.

'No.' And her voice revealed her own surprise that he knew.

'I heard it mentioned. Last night.'

She nodded slowly and those clear eyes pierced his, searched his. Challenged his. 'I guess we both have our secrets, Cameron Black.'

Then she walked away and he had no choice—no bloody choice—but to let her go.

Didi packed what she needed to take to Sydney. The rest she put into boxes and stored them where Cameron had put them before she'd arrived here. When she was done, she rang Amy and arranged to meet her at the Candle-side restaurant at six forty-five p.m. Then she let herself out of the apartment and walked. Anywhere. Everywhere. Until it was time to play the last scene.

When Cam arrived home to dress for dinner he found the place empty. Since she'd told him she'd meet him at the restaurant, he showered, dressed and arrived at precisely seven p.m.

As he stepped inside candles of every colour, size and shape imaginable illuminated the restaurant, giving it a cosy ambience. He didn't see Didi.

'Did you have a reservation, sir?' A neatly pressed waiter appeared with a couple of menus.

'I'm meeting Ms O'Flanagan. She doesn't seem to be here yet.'

The waiter nodded. 'Right this way.' He led Cam to a row of booths along the back wall. 'Here we are, sir.'

'No…this…' His voice disintegrated as familiar blue eyes so like his own looked back at him. Not dulled with drugs and depression and lack of interest as he remembered, but smiling and clear and alive. His heart spun a circle inside his chest, and somewhere deep inside him an ache that had embedded itself there for fourteen years dissolved.

'Hello, big brother.'

He slid into the booth before his legs crumbled beneath him. 'Amy.' His voice barely rose above a whisper. 'How...?'

'Didi set it up.' Amy poured a glass of water from a pitcher, set it in front of him.

His hand shook as he reached for the glass and lifted it to numb lips. He took a long slow sip to steady himself before he spoke. 'I don't understand.' How long had Didi known and kept it a secret from him? 'Doesn't matter,' he muttered, and slid along the seat to crush his sister against him. To inhale fresh citrus shampoo instead of stale booze and dope.

'Where *is* Didi?' he asked finally, still holding Amy, unable to let go.

'She stayed long enough to make sure I didn't run out on you.'

'She was here?' Cam looked about him, hoping to catch a glimpse of her.

Amy nodded. 'She's seen me outside your apartment. She caught up with me the other day and we had a long talk.' She twined her fingers with his, her eyes glinting in the candlelight. 'Now you and I are going to talk. Starting with the last time I saw you...'

* * *

'You love her, don't you.'

Cam's fingers tightened on his coffee cup. 'It's not that simple, Amy.'

'Yes. It is.' Amy's piercing blue gaze met his. 'You love someone you don't give up on them. Ever. You never gave up on me when you could have turned your back and walked away from a hopeless case.'

'This is different.' He stared into his coffee. 'Our relationship was only ever temporary.'

'So she says. You—'

He shook his head. 'She and her family have issues they need to sort out right now. She needs space.' But his heart was stirring to life in a way he'd never felt before. Was he ready to lay that heart on the line again?

Didi watched the reunion scene from a discreet distance through the restaurant's windows. In the dim candlelight Cameron was so focused on his sister, she knew he wouldn't notice her. But she could watch him for one more moment. A last glimpse through blurry eyes before she tore her gaze away and hurried to the waiting taxi outside.

Three hours later she was standing outside her

parents' Rose Bay mansion with two bulging suitcases. She punched in the security code and the high wrought-iron gates swung open on smooth oiled hinges. The panorama of lawn and paved driveway stretched in front of her like a marathon course.

Head high, Didi. She'd done what she'd set out to do. She was a success. There should be a trumpet fanfare for her return, or at least two people waiting on the steps with open arms.

So why did she feel like a little girl again trying to win her parents' approval?

The porch light winked on but the house was in darkness as she rolled her suitcases up the drive.

She rang the bell, heard it echo down the hall. A neighbour's dog barked and the sounds of night stirred in the nearby rose bushes.

Digging out her old key, she fitted it to the lock and let herself in. The door opened with its well-known scrape of wood against wood. She hoped they hadn't changed the security code as she tapped it in but no ear-splitting noise eventuated.

Familiar scents assaulted her nostrils. Mum's French perfume and the smell of old carpet. The Ming vase still sat on the antique rosewood table in the hall.

Nothing had changed.

Everything had changed.

She dragged her cases upstairs, hesitated at her parents' bedroom door. The familiar gold rose-sprigged quilt but the paintwork was new. She wrote a quick note, left it on the bed, then headed to her old room.

Everything was as she'd left it. Pink. It was like stepping back years and that feeling of suffocation with it. *No.* This time it would be different, she told herself, shaking it away, unzipping her case and dragging out her toiletries.

She was going to work here—in Sydney. The only contact with Cameron Black would be through email when she had pieces to deliver. Apart from that, she would not think about him, ever again.

Bathroom ritual complete, she climbed into bed...

The next thing Didi was aware of was daylight and her mother watching her with tears misting her grey eyes. Her complexion was smooth as ever, and only her mum's hair could look as if it had been salon-done first thing in the morning—even if it had a few more streaks of silver than the last time she'd seen her.

Her own eyes filled. 'Mum.'

'Didi. Is everything all right? You're not in any kind of trouble, are you?'

'No. I should have let you know I was coming, but it was…kind of sudden.' She pushed up, ran a hand over her own tousled hair. 'I had thought I might see you and Dad on Saturday night.'

'Saturday night, dear?'

'You didn't get my invitation?'

'We just got back from the airport a short time ago. We've been up to Hayman Island for a couple of weeks. What invitation? Oh, Didi…' Her voice dropped to a whisper, her eyes widened. 'Not…'

Didi waved a hand. Clearly her mother thought she'd been fool enough to fall in love and be dumped again. 'No, Mum. Nothing like that.' She swung her legs over the bed, optimism flooding through her as she realised her parents hadn't come to her special night because they hadn't known. 'The gallery opening. I was commissioned—extremely generously—to do the focal piece of artwork for a new gallery supporting local artists. Did Veronica tell you?'

'She mentioned something about your work. And that you were living with a man.' Only a glint of disapproval in her eyes. 'At a very exclusive address.'

Ah, that made it okay, then, Didi thought, resentment burning beneath her breast. A man like Cameron Black with his money and power would always be welcome here.

Not to her, he wouldn't. Because she wouldn't let him be.

'We've been waiting for you to tell us,' her mother said. She brushed a hand over Didi's hair.

A simple gesture. Only a mother's love could trigger the emotion that washed over Didi, threatening to drown her. 'I didn't think you'd want to know...'

Her mum smiled. 'Of course we want to know. *You* cut us out of your life, Didi.'

'No.' She shook her head, reached for her mother and was enveloped by the warm familiarity of her slender yet sturdy shoulders. Shoulders she desperately needed, she realised. 'I'm sorry we argued. I needed to find my own niche.'

'We know you did, dear. We'll talk about that later, with your father. Right now I'm more concerned with what's brought you home after all this time.' She leaned back, her grey eyes searching Didi's and pinpointing it with dead accuracy. '*He* did, didn't he? The man who gave you the chance you've been waiting for.'

'Oh, Mum. I made a mistake.' Again. She snapped a handful of tissues from the box on the bedside table. 'This time I really think my life's over.'

Her mum straightened, held Didi at arm's length and drilled her with that familiar don't-be-ridiculous-Didi look. 'That's nonsense. It's just started. You've finally achieved what you wanted. *How* much did you say he paid you?'

Didi smiled through her tears, this time not taking her mother's glare so literally. 'I didn't. But it's enough to live on comfortably for a bit while I work on more commissions. I've got orders for more and...'

'The world's opening up for you.'

She nodded, amazed at her mother's support. She'd taken such different impressions with her when she'd left. Hugged them to her for years.

'Tell you what, why don't you have a shower, dress and come down to the kitchen?' her mum said. 'We'll all have brunch. Rosita should be in shortly.'

'Rosita still works for you?' she said, wiping her nose.

'She does. I'll have her whip up one of those omelettes you always liked.'

'I can't get over the fact that you're taking this new career in art so well,' Didi said, between mouthfuls of fluffy egg mixture. 'You never showed any interest.'

'That's unfair, Didi.' Her mother sliced her toast into neat little squares. 'We were worried you wouldn't get anywhere and you'd be devastated; you were always so intense. So serious.'

'Your words were art was a nice little hobby but what was I going to do for a real job?'

Her father's hazel eyes met hers over the table. 'We were worried you wouldn't get where you wanted. We wanted you to have something to fall back on. Not many people can make a living as artists. You wouldn't discuss it, as I recall,' her father continued. 'The moment I mentioned university it was as if I'd suggested life imprisonment.'

'I wasn't interested in academia, Dad. I wanted to create.' *Come back when you're serious.*

'Yes. We know.' The only sounds were cutlery scraping china. 'So we let you stand on your own feet and waited for you to come back.' Another silence. 'It's taken this long. Always were a stubborn little thing.' Wistfulness laced his gruff words. 'This is your home,' he went on. 'Always was, always will be, for as long as you want. I hope you see that now.'

Emotion was washing through her—guilt, regret. Love. 'I do, Dad. I know I was a disappointment to you. I wished I could be like Veronica, but I just couldn't.'

'Not a disappointment, Didi. A puzzle maybe, but never a disappointment. Until you left. You walked away in anger, and you held onto it. That anger tainted your perception of what family is all about.' He shook his head. 'It was never give-and-take with you, was it?'

'I think I'm learning how to do that now, Dad.'

He raised one bushy grey eyebrow. 'Well, that's good to hear.' He wasn't done, she noted as he set his cutlery on his plate and his elbows on the table. She just knew he was going to—

'Now,' he said. 'About this man Veronica spoke about. Cameron Black, isn't it?'

CHAPTER FOURTEEN

CAM took in the view through the reinforced gate designed to keep lesser people out. Old money. The wealth you inherited and enjoyed and never truly appreciated. And there it basked in all its glory in Sydney's spring sunshine. The James O'Flanagan Residence.

He wasn't impressed. Cam had the assets to build better, and he'd earned every cent of that wealth himself with his own blood, sweat and tears. In spite of the low-life he was biologically descended from.

He'd done a lot of soul-searching over the past long torturous and lonely week. Katrina's prejudiced perception of others was wrong, and dangerous. The people Cam wanted to know judged others by their words and actions, not where they came from.

People like Didi.

She was smart and clever, caring and beautiful,

inside and out. One of a kind. And he wanted her in his life.

He sucked in a deep breath. The woman he'd come to convince was somewhere behind yonder stone façade.

But first he had to convince her father. Adjusting his jacket, he gritted his teeth against a sudden turmoil in his gut and buzzed the intercom. An employee, he assumed, answered with a hint of an Italian accent.

'My name's Cameron Black and I'm here to see Mr O'Flanagan.'

No, he wasn't expected, and yes, it was personal. He drummed his fingers against the pillar and waited. And waited.

Finally the gates swung open. He shouldered his bag and followed the smooth paved drive and its neatly trimmed hedge, aware that his movements were being tracked from one of those large glinting windows.

It wasn't the prospect of meeting James O'Flanagan that had his gut cramping, his mouth turning dry—he could face any man on an equal footing. But the thought of facing one small woman had him sweating inside his shirt in the chilly salt breeze blowing off the harbour.

Determination added extra length to his stride. He wasn't leaving until he'd seen Didi and said what he needed to say.

A middle-aged woman with long black hair tied back in a black ribbon showed him to a formal lounge room. She wore black trousers and a plain white blouse. He didn't sit as invited, but stood to attention looking out at a statue of Venus surrounded by never-ending lawn. A blue Sydney Harbour gleamed in the distance.

'Mr Black. Good morning.'

Cam swivelled to face the man with the crisp-edged voice. James O'Flanagan stood equal to Cam's own height with greying hair and a day's worth of stubble. For such a distinguished man he looked remarkably casual in a faded navy track-suit.

His expression was anything but. Cool astute eyes studied Cam. His mouth remained firm but relaxed; a man in full control of the situation. Unlike Cam, who'd grown unaccustomed to being on the receiving end of such powerful scrutiny—and it all had to do with the woman he'd come to see.

'Cameron.' Cam stepped forward, hand extended, feeling as if he were facing his own execution. 'Good morning.'

James's handshake was brief and firm. 'If you're expecting to see Didi, she and her mother are out shopping at present.'

'It's you I wanted to talk to. My apologies—I didn't inform you I was coming. Frankly, I wasn't certain you'd see me.'

James indicated a hard-backed brocade chair, then seated himself in a silk-covered recliner. 'Why's that?'

Why indeed? Cam sat, smoothing clammy palms over his trousers. He felt a tad light-headed. Must be the early flight coupled with a missed breakfast. And the fact that he hadn't had more than a handful of hours' sleep since Didi had left. 'Didi's mentioned me, I presume.'

'Both my daughters have mentioned you. The question still stands—why did you think I wouldn't speak to a man who's been seeing a lot of my daughter in recent weeks? Some might say he's the one man I *would* want to speak to.'

Cam fought the urge to clear his throat. The sound would be another sign of nerves James would pick up on. 'Didi and I parted…Didi *left* under difficult circumstances.'

For the first time, James's mouth allowed a hint of humour to tease the edges. 'Sounds appropriate—Didi's always been difficult.' He tapped a fist against his chin and the humour disappeared. 'When you say parted, are you talking personally or professionally? I was under the impression you were offering her a permanent spot in your gallery and intended liaising with her on future sales.'

'That's true. I will continue to give her all the support she needs, wherever she chooses to base herself.'

'So it's personal.' Leaning back, he folded his arms, ostensibly at ease, but those cool eyes remained steady on Cam's. 'What has Didi told you about our family?'

Diplomacy, here. 'To be honest, not a lot. During our conversations she told me she felt as if she never fitted in.'

James nodded as if it came as no surprise. 'She certainly didn't fit the criteria for your average child and that's not changed. Did she tell you that at five years of age she cut her mother's imported silk brocade curtains up to make matching dresses for herself and her doll?'

Cam had to smile. 'Curtains were mentioned.' Just not the cutting of them.

'We tried everything. Best schools, overseas with extended family. We suggested uni; she wouldn't discuss it.' He shook his head. 'Never could compromise, that girl. In the end we had to stand back and watch her go. To let her find her own place, make her own mistakes. Damn hard not interfering.'

His eyes drilled Cam's and Cam knew he was referring to their living arrangements—*previous* living arrangements. He nodded. 'Didi makes her own choices.'

'Did she talk about Jay?' James asked.

She was virtually stood up at the altar. The words still rang in his head. 'Jay...'

'It was a whirlwind romance—too serious too fast. They were engaged in a matter of weeks. A couple more weeks he was gone, back to his former girl. Broke Didi's heart.'

A knife twisted in Cam's belly—he'd hurt her too. 'Killed me to see my little girl so gutted.'

Cam nodded. He knew the feeling well. Didi's father wasn't what he'd expected. He genuinely cared about her, and she couldn't see it.

Still, James O'Flanagan might seem like a reasonable guy, but would Cam still be of the same opinion in the next few moments? He took a steadying breath and rose. If he didn't have command of the situation at least he could feel that he was in control of his own body. Except that the floor shifted like quicksand beneath his feet and someone was siphoning the oxygen from the room because it was suddenly airless.

But Cam's gaze was direct, his focus steady as he faced James. 'I need to tell you—'

The sound of women's chattering spilled through the doorway, cut off the moment the two women appeared.

Cam felt it all the instant he laid eyes on Didi—the sexual zing, as strong as ever, the flash of like recognising like. The quiet simmer of something stronger, something deeper—the foundation on which the rest was built.

She looked impossibly fragile and tiny in black leggings and an oversize windcheater, which had slipped off one shoulder exposing a turquoise bra strap and the glint of platinum chain he'd given her. He could smell her honey and almond scent from across the room.

Guilt rode him hard—that last evening he'd been so cool, so distant and unapproachable. He'd hurt her. He wanted to go to her, drag her into his arms, tell her he was sorry and never let her go, but he remained standing where he was.

Didi had heard Cameron's rumbling voice as she

reached the open doorway and everything inside her, every thought, had spun in a thousand different directions. *Why was he here?*

And then she forced herself to peek inside and there he was. Looking at her as if he wanted to eat her up. He wore fawn trousers and a deep blue suede jacket that accentuated his navy eyes. His white casual shirt was open at the neck revealing his tanned throat.

'Hello, Didi.'

Ah, the way he said her name...as if she were special. She knew better but her heart clawed its way up her throat along with a rising humiliation, her green eco-shopping bags slipping from her fingers as the strength drained out of her.

Didi had never been afraid of anything or anyone. Not until she'd met Cameron. Not until she'd fallen in love—really in love. Jay had been a mere rehearsal for the ultimate performance.

She was afraid now.

Afraid of what he might say. Afraid of what she might do. Of what she wanted to do. Even now, after the cool way he'd ended it, she wanted to rush right over and hurl herself into his arms and beg him to take her back.

'What are you doing here?' Pride kept her voice

firm and prevented her from running in the opposite direction. Pride and a fragment of that inner strength she thought she'd lost but managed to grapple back. 'I don't want you here, Cameron, nor do I want to talk to you. Anything we have to discuss we can do via a phone call or email.'

'Didi,' her father rebuked mildly. 'We brought you up better than that.'

'I'm here to talk to your father,' Cameron said.

She reached down, picked up her grocery bags. 'I'm going to put these in the kitchen. Please be gone when I get back.' Somehow she managed to walk away, hearing her mother say, 'Well...give Didi a moment. It's nice to finally meet you, Mr Black. What refreshments can I offer you?'

And Cameron's, 'Thank you, but I'm fine for now. Maybe later.'

Which left Didi with two alternatives. She could hide or she could show him she was managing just fine on her own. *As they'd agreed.* And whatever he had to say to her father...well, it couldn't be worse than what he *hadn't* said to her, could it?

Moments later she stood at the doorway. Her parents were seated, her mother saying something inane about the weather while Cameron stood to stiff attention in the centre of the room, his hands behind his back. He turned the moment she stepped into the room and met her gaze.

'You're still here,' she said.

His posture straightened, something flashed in his eyes. 'I'm not leaving yet. I have something to say.'

'Give the man a chance, Didi, for God's sake,' her father ordered.

Holding her head high, she crossed the room, conscious of Cameron's eyes tracking her the whole way. She stood rigid beside the sofa.

Cam dragged his eyes from Didi's and directed his gaze at her father. 'If you do a background check on Cameron Black you won't find me. Because my birth name isn't Black. It's Boyd. You may have heard of my father, Bernie Boyd. He was a known criminal and he died during a police chase.'

Silence rushed through the room. But James's expression didn't alter. He knew, Cam realised with a flash of insight. Of course he'd know. A man like James O'Flanagan would make it his business to know. He'd probably known the day after Veronica's visit.

Why hadn't he hunted Cam down?

'You never bothered telling me this stuff—why are you telling my parents?'

Cam turned at Didi's harsh voice. She was clutching her hands to her chest, her eyes grey and sharp, running him through.

'My father had a string of mistresses,' James said as if Didi hadn't spoken. 'He cheated on my mother for thirty years and drank himself into the grave. Does that make me a lesser man? I'd like to think not. I'd like to think I'm judged on my own merits.' He inclined his head. 'The same way I judge you, Mr Black. From what I've read about you, you made your fortune through sheer hard work. My enquiries have uncovered a man of persistence and integrity. A man I can respect and admire.'

Cam unclenched the hands he'd fisted behind his back. 'Thank you. I appreciate that.' The tightness in his chest eased, but only some.

He turned to the white-faced woman before him. He'd loved her the moment she'd voiced her low opinion of him loud and clear that first night. He just hadn't known it then. And she loved him too. She had to, he thought as something like panic skittered through him—his heart recognised hers.

Because love, he knew, was such a fragile experience—for both of them—he took a moment to soothe her with his eyes and spoke with a forced calm he didn't feel. 'Didi, why don't we go outside for a few moments? I'd like to talk with you privately—' he glanced at her parents '—if you'll excuse us?'

James nodded. 'Fine by me.'

'Why would I want to go outside with you?' she shot back in turbulent contrast. But he heard so much more behind the defiance and the stormy emotions in her eyes. Panic, pride. Passion.

'Because if you don't, I'll be forced to propose marriage to you in front of your parents and I really wanted to do that without an audience.'

Her breath hitched, her chin came up and shocked eyes stared back at him as twin spots of colour skidded along her cheekbones. 'You don't do commitment, why would you want to marry me? And you've just tried to convince them you're not suitable husband material.'

Would it always be this difficult with Didi?

Would he want her any other way?

'Maybe I've changed. Maybe I've had time to think about it. About us.' He pinned his gaze to hers, searching for the answer he wanted. Needed. The answer he knew was there. He was barely aware of Didi's parents making their way to the door.

Keeping his eyes on hers, he crossed the few steps separating them and wrapped his hands around her upper arms. 'I'm not asking them to marry me, I'm asking you. Damn it, Didi.' He gripped her arms tighter, gave a little shake. 'Look at the mess you're making of this.'

'*Me?*'

'Yes, you. You stubborn, difficult woman. I thought I'd ruin your reputation as an artist if people discovered my background and I was associated with you in a personal way. I didn't say what I wanted to ask you on that last night— what I'd planned to ask—because I didn't want to jeopardise your future. You'd worked so hard for success.'

'Yes. And you gave me the opportunity I needed.' She smiled for the first time. Only a tiny smile but it lit him from the inside out, spreading warmth through his limbs and hope in his heart.

He'd missed that smile. He'd missed her mess in the dining room, her clothes on the floor in his bedroom, her quick wit and charming idiosyncrasies. He'd missed her tousled hair tickling his nose as he slept.

'What had you planned to ask me?'

'I wanted to ask you to stay, to continue what we'd started.'

The smile faded. 'You mean our little arrangement. I would have said no.'

In the silence that seemed to stretch to eternity he heard birds, the sound of cutlery rattling somewhere in the house. The sound of his heart splintering into a million pieces. 'Would you mind telling me why?'

'Because it wouldn't have worked, Cameron.'

Desperation clawed its way back, his slippery hold on hope sliding through his fingers and they tightened once more. 'No, it wouldn't. I realised that when you walked out of my life. Because it wouldn't have been enough. Because I love you. And you love me. Which makes marriage our best option.'

A soft choking sound issued from her throat but he couldn't see her expression because her head dipped forward. Taking that as a promising sign— he refused to take it any other way—he grasped her hands and flattened them against his shirt.

'Or we could compromise,' he murmured against the top of her head. 'It wouldn't be my choice, but if we extended our arrangement by, say, sixty years or so... Exclusivity would be non-negotiable, however.'

Didi wanted to stand just like this, safe in Cameron's aura of warmth for ever. Breathing in his scent, watching the way his chest moved as he breathed, listening to his heart. He loved her. He'd let her leave because he thought her career meant more to her than him and he wanted to protect it.

With her palms against his hard-muscled belly, she lifted her gaze from the weave of his shirt to the V of flesh at his neck, his Adam's apple, the tiny patch of stubble he'd missed when shaving. The strong chin and those gorgeous lips. Last of all, she met his eyes, marvelling at the depth of emotion she saw there. Not clouded with denial the way she'd seen them on that last night, but naked and transparent, and, right now, tormented.

'If you think I'm going to live sixty years as your mistress, think again.'

'Di—'

'Shh.' She cut him off with a finger to his lips. 'Not another word. There's a place...' Entwining her fingers with his, she tugged him towards the door.

And what better place than the gazebo at the bottom of the garden where the wisteria perfumed the air and a butterfly chased a gentle breeze over the lawn?

She sat on the wooden seat, patted the space beside her. When he didn't sit, she looked up at him, shading her eyes from the sun's glare. All she could see was his silhouette; she couldn't read his expression and a little quiver of doubt rippled through her. Had she gone too far back in the house?

'Well?' she prompted in a very feminine co-quettish fashion she'd never heard come out of her mouth before. 'I've provided the privacy and the place. You mentioned something about a proposal... You've told, you've suggested, but you haven't *asked*.'

He moved out of the glare. His face looked un-usually harsh, the lines deeper around his thinned mouth, the sun bleaching the usual colour from his normally tanned skin. His voice was subdued when he said, 'Do you *want* me to ask, Didi?'

'I love the man you are,' she said softly. 'I love the way you've kicked adversity in the teeth and made something of your life despite all its obsta-cles. I love your compassion, your strength, your caring nature towards others. I love that you took me into your home when you didn't know me, even when I publicly embarrassed you that first night and gave me a chance to shine.

'I love *you,* Cameron Black, Cameron Boyd—whatever your name is, I love you.' She smiled up at him with all that love in her heart shining in her eyes. 'So yes, I want that very much.'

The smile he gave her in return was like the sun itself and she basked in the glow as it spread through her. 'Not quite yet,' he said, placing one foot on the seat beside her, leaning forward so she could smell his fresh soaped skin. 'You exploded into my life like a fireworks display, all noise and colour and energy. I'd never met any woman quite like you. A little pixie with no qualms about taking on the big guns and arguing—vociferously—for your fellow evictees. Losing your job in the process.'

'Pixie, huh?'

His smile widened as he danced his fingertips over her blonde spikes. 'I was absolutely enchanted. Still am. Always will be. But it was more,' he went on. 'You brought the spark that's been missing in my life. You taught me to look at things from a different perspective. We come from different worlds, Didi, and I want you to share your world with me the way I want to share my world with you. I don't want no-strings with you, Didi. I want nothing less than marriage, commitment, the works. But I'll compromise if I have to. If you'll have me.'

Tapping on the booted foot resting on the seat beside her, she smiled up at him. 'So get on with it—ask already,' she whispered.

He crouched in front of her and took her face in his palms. 'I said it before and I'll say it again, and I'll go on saying it for the rest of my life. I love you, Didi. Will you be my wife? You and me together for ever and a piece of paper telling us so.'

'Yes,' she breathed. 'Oh, yes.'

The kiss he pressed to her lips was the sweetest kiss she'd ever known, tasting of sunshine, tenderness and passion. Love. The kind that would last a lifetime. Twining her arms around his neck, she deepened the kiss, wanting to show him his feelings were returned multifold.

Finally, he drew away, pulled a little box out of the inside pocket of his jacket. 'I was hoping you'd say that. In fact I was counting on it.' He flipped the lid.

'Ah-h-h…' A solitaire diamond flanked on either side with two pink teardrop diamonds that matched the one on her necklace. She had to

press her fingers to her nose to stop it prickling.
'I couldn't have chosen anything better.'

It winked like fire in the sun as he slipped it on
her finger.

She looked at its sparkle of promise, then up at
him. At the depth of emotion in his eyes, at the
smile curving his lips. She watched as those lips
drew closer once more, her heart filled with love
and hope and happiness.

Then he was kissing her and her heart simply
overflowed. Here was rightness; this was what
she'd searched for. A man who could accept her
as she was, who valued her work and would work
beside her.

And not only did he value her work, he valued
her. With Cameron she was someone for whom
she would come an absolute first. She fitted in.
She belonged. She belonged with him in a way
she'd never belonged with her family.

When they finally drew apart and she settled
against his side, she asked, 'What would you have
done if my father's reaction had been different?'

'I'd have asked you anyway, then figured out a
way to get him onside. I was hoping you'd still
want me, baggage and all. We complement each
other. The people I want in my life don't care

about one's family background. I kind of figured you'd be the sort who'd thumb your nose at anyone who'd snub your art on account of who your husband is.'

'Damn right I would. But there's something I want to know and I never got a chance to ask you on that last night. Why did you name the gallery the Irene Black Memorial Gallery? You never mentioned her until your speech at the gallery opening.'

'Irene Black was my maternal grandmother. I can't condone what she did in disowning her daughter, but she gave me the kick-start I needed in the form of a single lump-sum deposit into my virtually non-existent bank account.

'Apparently she came to watch me one day when I was shovelling cement on a construction site as an eighteen-year-old. She tracked my movements over the months, saw how I was trying to cope with Amy and made contact.

'I only met her that once. She died a week later. Alone. I was robbed of knowing my grandmother. I changed my name to hers in her honour.'

'I'm sorry, Cameron.' She touched the tiny crease that had formed between his brows and kissed the shadows from his eyes. 'But you have family now. Amy. Me. My parents. And, for better or worse, Veronica.'

'Yes.' He nodded, shook off the melancholy. 'Speaking of for better or worse, in your family I guess it's the big white society wedding?'

Not if Didi could help it. She smiled at him. 'What would you prefer?'

'The two of us and a marriage celebrant.'

She felt a grin coming on. 'So we'll compromise. It'll still be the big white dress and wedding cake, but we'll invite only our immediate family and have it here in the gazebo. How does that sound?'

He kissed her lips. 'Perfect.'

EPILOGUE

Melbourne, two months later

'WHERE are we?' Didi's hands curled over the blindfold Cameron had insisted she wear for the drive he'd promised would be short but was taking far too long.

'Patience, Mrs Black, we're nearly there.'

Finally the car slowed and stopped. She could barely wait until Cameron opened the door. Then he swept her up against his chest. She could feel the sun on her cheeks, hear birdsong and someone mowing their lawn, kids shouting and the rrrrch of their skateboards as they sped past.

He stopped.

'What?' she demanded.

'I can't decide where...'

'You always were the sort to take too long to think things over. Enough.'

'And you're always too impatient.'

The outdoor noises faded, the warmth of the

sun on her skin cooled and she knew he was taking her indoors. But where?

He stopped again, set her on her feet. 'Ready?'

She dragged the blindfold off. And looked straight at her Temptation. 'You said it was sold. It *was* sold—you gave me a very large cheque to prove it.'

'I couldn't bear to part with it,' he murmured behind her. 'What do you think—should it go here or in the bedroom?'

'You mean...this place is...'

'Ours,' he said. 'Yours and mine. It's home.'

Home. Warmth geysered up inside her.

She spun around, taking in the room with its mish-mash of homey-looking furniture. Furniture that looked vaguely familiar. Furnishings and décor she'd commented on in the numerous *House & Garden* magazines Cameron had taken to reading of late.

She turned to the window overlooking a backyard and cottage garden crammed with a kaleidoscope of colours. A place to breathe, to watch the seasons come and go. 'But we have your apartment.'

'You once said you couldn't bear to live in an apartment.'

'No garden, fresh air, sky or pets. I remember. But—'

He took her hand and led her towards a closed door. 'Come with me.'

When he opened the door Didi saw a modern kitchen with just about every modern appliance ever made. And in the corner—

'Charlie!' Surrounded by four mewling kittens.

'Charlotte,' Cameron corrected as she rushed over to fondle him...her.

'Oh, I've missed you so so much.' She stroked the silky fur, careful not to disturb the nursing babies. 'No wonder I thought he—*she*—was putting on weight. I thought it was my care and attention.'

She stretched up on tiptoe to twine her arms around Cameron's neck. 'She'll always be Charlie to me. Thank you.'

'You're welcome. We have a big backyard that'll accommodate as many pets as you want. Within reason,' he suggested.

She smiled up at him. 'Five's good. Although maybe we could get a dog some time...' The kiss that inevitably followed was long and lingering. 'Are you sure you want to give up apartment living?' she said when at last he drew back.

'I'm sure. Circumstances change. Now we need somewhere with more space—a place for you to create your masterpieces. A garden for Charlie and her brood and room to grow...'

'Speaking of growing...' Didi felt a naughty smile coming on as she drew him back to the living room with its plump green sofa. Naughty for twelve-thirty on a working day. But then, that was becoming something of a habit lately. She looked pointedly at her Temptation mural. 'If we're going to create our own little masterpiece together...we should get started.' Pulling him down on the sofa she began undoing buttons.

'There's a nice soft bed you haven't seen yet,' he murmured, helping her.

'We'll get to that,' she told him. 'Later.'

And they did.

Much later.

Cameron took the rest of the afternoon off.

* * * * *